CHOICES

FROM THE

AMERICAN REVOLUTION

by

Kim Kacoroski

Cover art illustrations by Kim Kacoroski, Phillipe Velasquez, and Masha Tatarintsev

Visit the author website:
http://kimkacoroski.com

ISBN: 978-1-947036-08-6 (Paperback)

Version 2017.23.03

Book Four of Flight Series

Choices from the American Revolution IV

Other Books in the Flight Series

Flight from Oblivion I

Eagle's Flight in the American Revolution II

Flight of the Ascendants from the American Revolution III

Bridges before the American Revolution V

Testimony VI

Books in the Oblivion Series

Escape from Oblivion I

Beyond Oblivion II

Oblivion's Edge III

Oblivion's Deal IV

Flight from Oblivion V

Books in the Camelon Series

The Promise of Camelon I

The Dragons of Camelon II

History of the World According to the Druids III

New Beginnings IV

The Kingdom of the Golden Tara V

Testimony VI

Chapter One

Blanket me with the snow

Of a love long lost

So that the chill of surrender

Never steals the value of a dream

Made real by a war once fought

On the earth where my frozen feet stood

Immobilized by a path

Etched by the certainty

Of having no place left to go.

As final as the cold swirling around me

I felt until I could fell no more

Numbed by spent experience

Still moving in the darkness

Beckoning me to continue.

Blankets-------

Kim Kacoroski © 2/10/1997

1809 Alabama, USA

THE SMALL CHILD pulled a white daisy from the ground beneath her bare toes. Rising no higher than her ankles, small green plants studded the leveled brown terrain. Her tiny hands remaining clasped around the stem as she looked at the horizon. Dropping her focus, she cocked her head and listened for the source of the thunder in the distance. She raised her head and glanced at the western horizon. A vibration in the earth pulsed beneath the arches of her feet.

A lone rider appeared from the thicket and quickly dismounted fifty yards from the child.

Where's Bilbo?" the horseman asked as he approached the child.

She stared at the man clutching his chest with one arm as he hobbled a few steps from the horse. He motioned her to resume her play after she answered. The rider knew the name of the hauflin who inhabited the small house by the riverbank. The river bore the name of hauflin, the one ferrying souls to another realm called the Mid-Earth. Though the seasons changed the nature of the river, Bilbo followed his meandering course. Still holding the flower, the little girl raised her hand and pointed at a nearby creek. "There."

The dark-haired man followed her direction and hurried toward a sandy embankment. A tall, slender woman emerged from a dense portion of the woods. Carrying a basket of wild sorrel in one arm, she silently waved at the child, who forgot about the wandering horseman and ran to give her the daisy. Accepting the daisy from the child's chubby hands, the woman stabled her infant under one arm and knelt to look at eyes of the toddler. Watching the man descend into the crevasse bordering the river, she remarked to the child, "Pierre is escaping to the MidEarth. He wants to consult Bilbo."

Swirls of white vapor surrounding Pierre as he made his way down a rocky, steep slope to the water's edge. He lost his footing and grabbed a protruding tree root to stop his plunge into the river. After he regained his balance, he looked around for Bilbo, the caretaker of the MidEarth. The fog became denser and tiny fairies darted in the misty air, lighting their flight with a series of sparkles like fireflies. Taking a deep breath, he coughed slightly as he clutched his chest and spat blood at the dirt beneath his feet.

Although, he could not see him, Pierre sensed Bilbo's presence. Nonverbally, he confided to the hauflin about the attack on the naval station. The hauflin replied about Pierre's rendezvous with destiny. He promised to hide Pierre so that the lynch mob did not destroy his soul. Years ago, the United India company attacked Pierre's regimen and killed some of his adopted children. His wife, Nicole, mourned their loss. Traitors at the naval station disagreed with Pierre on the issue of human trafficking, which had taken the lives of the children. Though Bilbo had given Pierre an aquila, the Council of Rome invaded the fort and captured Pierre. They announced their intention to poison the planet for their alien sponsors.

Under gunfire, Pierre escaped home to alert Nicole and his son, Double J, otherwise known as Jean Jacque by his Apache mother. Double J's mother died defending Switzerland and Pierre learned of his son a few years after wedding Nicole, who had informed him of his young son Jean. Having adopted the name of the French bankers funding Napoleon as an alias, Pierre called his sons Jean Lafitte. All five of Pierre's sons by different women used the name Jean Lafitte as they worked with the US Naval Academy in Annapolis.

Pierre emerged from the misty air moments later and greeted the threesome. "Hello, Nancy and young Sara." Nodding at the babe tucked under Nancy's arm, he took a deep breath and found his balance as he shifted his weight from one artificial leg. His shoulders dropped with fatigue from the long journey. Sitting down on the verdant carpet, Pierre explained, "Napoleon's sponsors attacked the Gulf coast. Bilbo has the gold crown from their icon."

"I heard from Nicole that the Sicilian pirates assumed control of the naval station," the woman replied, clutching her children close. As she lifted the toddler to her bent knee, Nancy quickly changed the subject, "My husband, Issac, owned the adjacent property. I came to deliver our son, who he asked me to name, Abraham. Thomas Lincoln thinks that I am visiting relations in Kentucky and I must leave early tomorrow."

Exhausted from the war and travels, Pierre rolled on the ground and rested. Looking up at the clear, sapphire-blue sky, he heaved several deep breaths and fell asleep without further discussion. A few tears streamed from his closed eyelids and left shiny, aqueous crystals that twinkled in the brilliant light of spring. Nancy left his to attend to her children's needs and prepare for her return to the Lincoln cabin. After spending the night in the hut of her former family, she departed for Kentucky before the sun rose. Nancy took the road opposite the grassy clearing. Her wide-eyed daughter glanced in Pierre's direction before the horse swerved onto the main trail.

Looking down at the child sitting in front of her, Nancy responded, "Pierre's had a rough ride. Bilbo will hide him."

In the morning, the couple living in Nancy's hut finished their chores and walked over to the clearing where Pierre spent the night. When they failed to rouse him from his slumber, the man gently touched Pierre's left hand, which laid beside him and remained open to the skies above.

"The body is cold," the man commented to the woman standing nearby. He lightly shook Pierre's body before leaning over his chest to listen for a heartbeat. Looking up at the woman beside him, he remarked, "His heart stopped. He's dead."

"Oh, my!" the woman exclaimed. "Quick, get the body into the house, so we can hide it from the authorities."

As the couple discussed preparations for the secret burial, a light mist circled toward them. Emanating from Bilbo River, the cloud vapor enveloped the deceased and hid the couple from view. The man gazed at the swirling white stream and noted that the visibility had rapidly decreased to the length of his elbow. Making the most of the protective cover, he grabbed the body from the shoulders and attempted to drag it across the field. The woman paused for a moment and sniffed the air. Straightening in her stance, she raised her head and decided, "Wait. It's Gilderoy and Paisley."

Two glow-in-the-dark, fluorescent Sea Dragons emerged from the thickening mists. Rising almost eight feet from the ground, the shimmering creatures beamed at the couple. Gilderoy, the brilliant blue Sea Dragon bowed his head with a makeshift ceremonial air. Paisley, the psychedelic-paisley-patterned Sea Dragon with the yellow jewel in the middle of his forehead, erupted into a shit-eating grin and commented, "It's another new beginning."

"You two certainly know how to put out a fire," the man retorted, putting the body down as he wiped water droplets off his forehead with his paisley-patterned handkerchief.

"We know how to start one, too," Gilderoy interjected. He raised his head slightly and puffed a golden flame above the a small assembly. Extinguished by the aqueous clouds, the fire transformed into a whirl of sparks before disappearing into the gray haze. "Remember, we started a revolution at Bowling Green, Kentucky. We carried the movement over from Scotland, when King Dewi of Wales passed over."

"Yes, the father of Nancy's newborn descended from Dewi's line," Paisley added. "Pierre knows the story."

Gilderoy cleared his throat and interrupted his cohort, "Remnants of Constantine's left-behind armies in Britain intend to finish killing all traces of Camelon and Avalon, the only civilizations resisting the invasion."

With a distinguished grunt, Paisley cut Gilderoy short. He added, "The stray Roman emperors made a deal with the devil. The devil wants to destroy Earth by 2012." After pausing for a moment, he nodded toward the dead man's horse. As the wild mustang emerged through an opening in the mists, Paisley asked rhetorically, "What do you think happened to Mars?"

Glancing toward the hidden sky, the man resumed his position near the body and began tugging. "Let's get going."

The woman shrugged and decided, "There's no time to waste."

The mustang snorted and shook its head at the dead horseman lying on the ground. Rather than entice the beast into service, Gilderoy disrupted the man's efforts and pocketed the body in his pouch. Then he turned abruptly, wandering in the direction of the couple's cabin. Paisley strode after Gilderoy, while the couple followed behind with the mustang.

At the cabin, Paisley took the body from Gilderoy and placed the deceased on the wood floor of the main room. Gilderoy stepped away. "Send someone for his next-of-kin."

"There's a woman who knows him in Mobile," Paisley interjected. "We met his son, Jean Jacque, a few years ago. The mother leads the parades."

A knock at the door interrupted the discussion. Startled by the rap, the man looked for a way to hide the body and dragons. The mustang outside whinnied in acknowledgement at the intruder. The sound relaxed the man and he opened the door with a calm air.

The young man walked in the room after patting the mustang in greeting. He stared at Pierre's body and introduced himself. "Hi, I'm his son Double J."

"I go by the name of Thomas Owen. I've been studying with Justice John Marshall to become a judge. Patrick Henry taught me how to read before he passed away."

The woman nodded at the man and suggested. "Check his jacket for documents."

After removing the jacket and shirt, the man exposed a thick layer of bandages wrapped around Pierre's chest. Noticing the pool of blood contained by the layers of bandages, the woman grabbed a bucket and several rags. As she collected the liquid before it covered the floor, she commented, "Pierre took a bullet."

"Around these parts, we get plenty of arrivals with hidden wounds. They die once they come out of shock."

"His wife didn't see the injury when she helped him on his horse. There's a fake boot on his left leg."

"I see," the woman responded. "Only next-of-kin would know about the fake leg."

Meanwhile, Paisley left the cabin for Bilbo River, where he summoned a Sea Dragon to send word to the seer in Mobile. A day after the burial, the woman and Jean Jacque arrived from Mobile. The group met the newcomers near the thicket as they dismounted. She hugged Double J in greeting. With her arm around her nine-year-old son, she announced, "It's a new beginning. Jean Jacque, this your time."

"Come with me to Galveston," Double J requested. "I work with Sam Houston there."

Stepping back, the seer glanced at her son for a response. The vapor from Bilbo River covered the area in a thick gray smoke, making wayward travel impossible. Only those with a sense of purpose and direction could pursue the paths laced through the swamps and woods. Gilderoy approached the gathered crowd. "We shifted our focus to the US government rather than privateering. The attack from Sardinia and Sicily exposed the Eagle's naval forces."

"Did Cornelia leave already?" the seer asked.

"She left an hour ahead of Nancy. Cornelia assisted with the delivery of her son, Abraham. She's been working as a cook for Thomas Lincoln, the guard for Lexington's prisoners-of-war."

After the refugees from the American Revolution arrived at Pottinger's Station in Kentucky, pirates from skull and bones fraternity captured the survivors. They shanghied some to China, while conscripting the others. Posing as Puritans and Quakers, the associates of William Penn's fraternity hid their operations by distancing themselves from those with dark-skin, whom they hired. Cornelia Mitchell, a descendant of the French officer Cornelius Mitchell, accompanied Toussaint L'Ouverture's aide to negotiate with the US president. Sardinians sponsored Bonaparte's ally and pitted him against Adams's administration. The same matriarch-led fraternity that demanded the head of John the Baptist, an ancestor of Nancy's departed husband, constructed institutions resembling the structures of ancient Rome. In contrast to a new beginning, the heinous operation surfaced on the American continent and cast shivers in the bravest communities. Cornelia recognized the treachery and remained in the US, while supporting Toussaint's efforts in Jamaica as the betrayal played out, eventually taking the life of Toussaint. Thanks to Cornelia, Toussaint remained a posthumous thorn in the side of the Bonaparte operation, which she forced underground. The secret life of Cornelius Mitchell eluded Thomas Lincoln, who worked with the Russells to reseed themselves in the leading families of the conquered natives. Considered a villain by the Plymouth settlement, Captain John Smith attempted to force his way into Powhatan's leadership. Only those who didn't write the books knew the truth. Histories on paper never told the story of the exploits of the Transylvania Land Company. Powhatan, the father of Pocahontas, lost his coat, but kept his family. Plymouth authorities returned Captain John Smith to England in chains. The British company housed his mantle in an institution of higher education.

After covering up the murder of Meriwether Lewis to avoid a war with the sponsors of the land-grabbers, the Jefferson administration gave way to a group of occultists called the Federalists. The Templar knights, who manufactured the Shroud of Turin in Sardinia, repeated the sorcery of Constantine's mother. Instead of using a relic of a cross to captivate their subjects, the empire resorted to cloth, as they sought greater control of the transactions on the Silk Road.

President Madison rose from a Roman temple erected in the foothills surrounding Monticello, the architectural marvel that put Jefferson in debt to enemies of a free nation. With a secret fraternity, he conspired with the Roman Empire for the upcoming War of 1812. Though he succeeded in burning down the White House, the Eagles stopped the invasion.

Chapter Two

CORNELIA GREETED NANCY Hanks at the front door to Thomas Lincoln's cabin. The five-week old infant remained concealed in the folds of her garments. Sara stood beside her and tugged lightly on one of the folds of her dress. After helping Nancy deliver her son in Alabama, Cornelia quickly returned to the Lincoln settlement in Missouri. She met with several Zuni from Dixieland in the surrounding back hills. Thomas Lincoln never questioned her whereabouts, because the woodsman appreciated the regularly scheduled meals and preferred being alone.

Like Daniel Boone, Thomas Lincoln served as an agent for the Transylvania Land Company. After the Hudson Bay company murdered Meriwether Lewis, relatives implemented an occult settlement in the Pacific Northwest to conquer the native tribes. After renaming one of the mountains for a British officer and another for the mother of the Roman Emperor, who destroyed native settlements in Camelon, Avalon, and Marlboro. They joined forces with the same Roman forces which had demanded the head of John the Baptist, a son of a chieftain with relations under guard in Rome. In accordance with Revere's copper engraving of the Lexington Battle, the first official conflict of the American Revolution, the companies cast the dark alchemical die for rewriting the history of the continent. Like Boone's Lexington in Kentucky, the main road leading to

Mount Saint Helens and Mount Rainer bore the name Lexington's Bridge. Boone established another enterprise closer to the waterway called Boones Ferry. The city nearby earned the named Battle Ground, and served as the extermination camp for displaced natives.

Cornelia ushered Nancy inside the house and through the main room. Stepping briefly behind the door to the kitchen, Cornelia produced several biscuits and handed them to Sara. A dark-skinned older man appeared in the room and took Sara's free hand. Stooping over the small child, he remarked, "Mr. Lincoln hunts in the woods. We expect him back tomorrow morning."

"I've kept the hearth warm. Smoke still hangs in the air over the stall," Cornelia continued.

Nancy hurried out the back door toward the stable. Cornelia followed her and roused the chickens into a cry that would mask the infant's low whimper. Sara followed her mother inside the small room near the barn. The man held the door open wide as Nancy entered and confronted the surroundings, which reflected the passing of the man she once loved. Sitting in a rocker near the hearth, she began nursing the baby as the man closed the door. Cornelia knocked and let herself in the room. She held a basket with a pot of warm porridge and biscuits and placed it on an end table.

"How are the Zuni?" Nancy asked, lifting her head and staring at Cornelia.

Without replying, Cornelia gave her a small bill. Nancy looked down at the note in her hand. An establishment in New Orleans minted the currency for Dixieland, a section of Utah once inhabited by the Anasazi. Considered sacred territory by the Native Americans, Dixieland served as the return to the post-Eden culture of Gondwanaland. The Zuni purchased many of Issac's things and paid Nancy for the goods with the denomination of the Iroquois Confederacy. After the Anasazi left with the extraterrestrials, the Apaches took over operations, extending their influence from the Gulf of Mexico. They worked with the Miamis from Florida, the Lacerta on the West coast, and the Iroquois Confederacy. When Spanish conquistadors followed Ponce de Leon on the Continent, the Native Americans hid their gold and continued working with the Dragon flyers from Europe. Governor Galvez ran supplies to the Eagles during the American Revolution and developed a currency separate from the US dollar with the dark occult symbolism embedded into its pyramidal economic associations. Named for the scared territory formerly inhabited by the Anasazi, the Dixie paper currency replaced the gold of the seven major cities of Cibola.

While Benjamin Franklin's estranged legal wife weaved dark occultism into the currency of the United India company, Benjamin Franklin's common-law wife established the Dixie as the monetary system for the Eagles, which included fleeing European monarchies and Native Americans. They conducted their trade with this note printed by banks in New Orleans, where Pierre and his privateers cultivated cotton for refugees from the American Revolution. This endeavor disengaged them from the treacherous dealings which characterized trading on the Silk Road and Spice Routes. Sidestepping the maneuvers of the Columbus company, which enslaved the locals on any continent, the Eagles thrived under the circumstances.

Nancy examined the red note by the light of the fire as she nursed Abraham. People told her that the design fit the red rocky terrain known as Dixieland. The bill represented good will, which often proved more valuable than gold. She stashed the bills away for the future of her children. They would have friends for as long as they lived. Like most mothers, Nancy possessed ambitions and wished for Abraham to follow in the footsteps of Thomas Owen. As the Transylvania Land Company seized more territory through brutal exploitation, John Marshall made it clear that more lawyers would be needed. Though categorized as a Federalist, Marshall had stared down the devil and stopped Daniel Webster from selling out any hard won gains through Annapolis, which many still considered the capital of the new nation.

A time of lies and subterfuge, agents from the Transylvania Land Company infiltrated the settlers and Native Americans to melt the Iroquois Confederacy into soldiers called Grays. These mind-control units created havoc and subjected the planet to alien invasion, the same entities which made ancient Greece and Rome insane. Cells of Grays patterned themselves from a unit in Bedford, England. After having successfully ruled the seas and pirated commerce with a single terrorist named Drake, the United India company continued the tradition long perfected since the days of the Spartan warriors in ancient Greece. The Vikings laced their trade routes with such programmed soldiers and promoted the Crusades with assistance from the insanity of ancient Rome.

Another knock on the door announced the entrance of two Zunis, which could easily be mistaken for local tribes in the Missouri frontier.

"Where are you going next?" one of the natives questioned.

"Thomas Lincoln is on the run with his prisoners," Cornelia answered. "Gilderoy and Paisey are keeping him out of Bowling Green, Kentucky, though he has a station in nearby Elizabethtown. He mentioned that he plans to stay in Missouri and work with the Sacred Heart base from France." Turning away from Nancy, she confided to the Zuni, "The French financiers want to carve the heart out of the population and enslave the zombies."

Chapter Three

AFTER THE ZUNI left, Cornelia gathered the kitchenware and returned to the main house. Out of the corner of her eye, she recognized an agent from the Lewis and Clark expedition as he emerged from the woods. She left the house under the care of Edward, the manservant, and rushed to greet the newcomer.

Dressed in the fringed buckskin pants and jacket of the local frontiersmen, the agent stepped back into the dense woods when Cornelia approached. Ushering her closer to him, he mentioned in a hushed voice, "The Grays call themselves Confederates. They drive the Native American uprisings near the Great Lakes. Stay here. Let the religious fanaticism runs its course."

"Who's leading the facade?" Cornelius asked, stepping behind several bushes for cover.

"Captain Heald. He worked with Thomas Lincoln in Indiana and has replaced Captain Whistler at Fort Dearborn. Wilkinson's agents put Heald in charge. Now the Shawnee have the same prophets that inspired Caesar's madness."

"The British companies will use the ploy to officially gain control of the capital at the District of Columbia," Cornelia observed. "Madison will hand the reins right over."

"That is the power of a lie," the agent remarked. "The coverup for what happened at Lexington proved short-lived. Those protesting the betrayal now have a voice. Though compromises have been made, the nation hasn't fallen into alien hands. Even Rome fell before planetary control became absolute."

Paisley appeared from behind the agent. In contrast to the seriousness of the discussion, his psychedelic colors lent a comical air to the atmosphere. Cornelia shielded her eyes and ignored him. The Sea Dragon did his best to put Cornelia and the agent at ease. Munching on a stash of wild greens, the fluorescent shimmering Sea Dragon hid behind a large shrub with a few fairies to avoid casting a glare. Between bites, he interjected a running commentary. "No problem. The O'Connor armies from Pennsylvania will catch up with Thomas Lincoln. Annapolis intends to send a crew to Fort Dearborn to push out Heald and the programmed Native Americans. It may not be pretty, but we will win in that part of the country."

Both Cornelia and the agent quieted and stared at Paisley, who continued to munch noisily on wild edibles like an overgrown caterpillar. Leaving the agent and the Sea Dragon, she hurried back to the house. Cornelia arrived in time as the dogs erupted in a chorus of barks to greet Thomas Lincoln, who slowly rode his horse inside the stable. Rising his head he looked for signs of his prisoner living in the nearby sod hut. Satisfied with seeing the smoke rising from the chimney, he dismounted and headed for his home instead of concerning himself with the occupants. Cornelia nodded at Edward, while he carried a tray in the next room. For a brief moment, their eyes made contact. Cornelia saw the glint in the eyes of the British man, assuring her that he could handle the temper of Thomas Lincoln. Before he strode through the swinging door separating the kitchen from the main room, Edward grabbed a small bottle and added a few drops to Thomas's whiskey. Exhausted from his recent journey, Thomas soon fell asleep on his bed beside the fire.

Time passed quickly and a messenger arrived a few days later. Unable to bring himself to check on the young family in the hut, Thomas accepted the telegram, which had been intercepted by Cornelia's network. With a slight shrug and toss of his head, Thomas repacked his bag, while Edward retrieved his horse from the stable. As he positioned himself in the saddle, Thomas glanced at the hut. Curls of smoke blew from the chimney and hung in the mists over the woods. Taking a deep breath, he smiled contentedly to himself and whipped his horse toward the road in front of the house.

Cornelia watched him leave as she peered out the solitary window in the kitchen while washing the breakfast dishes. Edward left to check on the young family. Cornelia put away her apron and saddled her horse in the stable. Taking the opposite direction on the road, she rode into Saint Louis and directed her horse through the backstreets. Cornelia stopped at the back of the main store in town. As she tied her steed to the post, the head grocer stepped outside and descended the steps. Calling to her softly, the Englishman hurried to her. He affectionately kissed Cornelia's cheek and took Cornelia by the arm. Together they climbed the stairs leading to the stock piled high inside the wooden structure. A white cotton curtain separated the stockroom from the store. Peering at the aisles through the openings at both ends of the cloth, Cornelia strained her neck briefly before turning her gaze to the business of the stockroom.

"How many rifles?" she asked.

"One thousand two hundred and forty-three," the grocer answered. "We can't let Madison turn us over to the British company. We start drilling tomorrow, while the Sacred Heart choir practices."

"Is Brother Willard keeping watch in the steeple tower?"

The grocer nodded in reply. He selected three of the rifles and wrapped them for Cornelia to take back to Nancy's hut. Covering the arms with parchment, he raised his head and questioned, "How's her baby?"

"Looks like he'll grow to be as tall as his daddy," Cornelia commented while knotting strings around the brown paper.

Then she lugged the package over her shoulder and exited. Reaching the hut early in the afternoon, Cornelia announced her presence and let herself in the door. Nancy stood near a small pot hanging in the hearth, while Sara rearranged play sticks on the dirt floor. Cornelia peeked at the infant in the cradle, which had been erected in Thomas's absence. Nancy took the parcel from Cornelia and hid the unwrapped guns in a kitchen cupboard. Without knocking, Edward entered the hut and stood in the middle of the room. He looked around unceremoniously and stood firmly on the ground. Stomping one foot, he listened for a hollowness beneath the floor. He scraped away the dirt and lifted the top of the trap door. One by one, the group descended the stairs into a cellar. Nancy carried young Abraham in her arms and made her way carefully into the small dark room. Shelves of books lined the rock walls, which became visible only by the soft flickering light of Cornelia's lamp. Nancy pulled a particular text from the literary array and cradled it with the infant. She ascended the stairs and disappeared in the room above, while the others grabbed a few token treasures. Even little Sara found something for her amusement. A picture book of exotic animals caught her eye. Returning to the room above the cellar, they Nancy seated in her rocker, studying a book on medicine. Fully awake, the baby stared wide-eyed as the group reassembled and recovered the trap door. Each possessed a collection of books on their favorite subject. Edward held several history books in his hands and left to read in his favorite chair in the main house. Cornelia stayed with Nancy and began reading one of her novels.

Making the most of her captivity, Nancy learned enough from the medical texts to discreetly consult for the locals who sought her advice during Thomas's frequent extended absences. When the War of 1812 arrived, she used her Dixie earnings to pay for her family's passage to Bowling Green, Kentucky, a place she knew Thomas and his gang feared. Edward burned the hut to the ground after removing the treasures from the cellar. Thomas believed Nancy and her family had died in the fire and refused to look for them. Cornelia dried her fake tears as she related the fabrication. Edward handed Thomas his altered whiskey, which never brought any complaints. Thomas merely sipped the concoction and went to bed early. Cornelia remained with Thomas another year before moving on. Edward went with Thomas to Indiana, where he established a farm.

Cornelia visited Nancy often at Bowling Green. The Sea Dragons continued to hold boule matches in the fields and entertain discussions on the revolution from the sidelines. The revolution reached intergalactic depths as the Sea Dragons sought to restore the earth's spirit.

During one brilliant green spring down, Cornelia took her turn on the bowling lawn and attempted to distract Gilderoy from his next roll.

"Now what is the revolution about?" she asked, watching Sara show her toddling younger brother how to gather the white daisies strewn across the meadows.

Gilderoy raised his bowling ball and almost keeled over. Fortunately, Paisley composed himself and answered while his brother regained his balance. He said confidently with a twinkle in his azure-blue eyes, "It is not about winning or losing; the revolution is about how you play the game."

Having overheard Paisley's statement, Abraham dropped his fistful of daisies and clapped his tiny hands. He echoed to the group, "Play. Play."

Cornelia chuckled at the sight of the toddler cheering on the Sea Dragons. She remarked, "That young one is going to grow up and be a vampire hunter just like my daddy."

"Yes, your father studied from some of the best. Captain Davy sent one of his musketeers to Jamaica to support Toussaint's efforts in Santa Domingo," Gilderoy said, shifting his weight from one foot to the next as he aimed the ball.

"This maneuver allowed Toussaint to keep his promise to keep Jamaica out of the revolution in the Caribbean," Paisley observed with a shrug. "With its own army of musketeers, Jamaica calmly infiltrated the Spanish legions of the Columbus company and formed allies with disenchanted European royals."

The sound of thunder accompanied Gilderoy's throw across the grass. Rather than become intimidated by the performance, the toddler laughed and clapped his little hands together. Sara took her brother by the arm and gently lead him to the thicket, so that he would not get hit by a wild pitch. Cornelia lifted her head and tossed her bowling ball. It silently landed near Gilderoy's without any fanfare.

Cornelia sternly confronted Gilderoy and Paisley, "Quit trying to impress the children."

"Are you trying to steal our thunder?" Paisley asked solemnly.

"Life is not just another show," she retorted.

"That is why you are in charge of this particular youngster," Gilderoy responded.

Cornelia bowed her head and looked down on the ground at the collection of bowling balls underneath her feet. "Are you inferring that it is only a matter of time before Lincoln's associates catch up with Nancy.

Paisley lifted one of the balls to his chin and firmly nodded at Cornelia. "They will eventually be able to get past our thunder. The young ears are becoming mute."

Cornelia watched his ball roll quietly over the grass and stop near hers. Studying the arrangement on the field, she remarked, "You were testing the children." Straightening her back, Cornelia acknowledged, "Nancy was right to wait out the War of 1812 at Bowling Green." Her shoulders arched slightly as she eerily eyed the Sea Dragons, "The place brings everyone back to their senses."

"Precisely," Gilderoy admitted while timing his next windup. He stared at the court before him without saying a further word.

Having realized another golden moment of silence, Cornelia shrugged at Paisley. The Sea Dragon beamed softly, welcoming her thoughts that would continue their discussion. "As the violent carnage mounts, it becomes even more important to hear life's subtleties.

"Yes, Gilderoy is not the only philosopher in the game," Paisley said as he surveyed the lawn for his next throw.

Nancy appeared on the green from behind them. Intent on their play, no one had seen her approach. She added to the conversation, "As Issac always said, *we mustn't lose our sensitivity.*"

"I'll remember that," Cornelia promised, looking away from Nancy. The starkness of the discourse empowered her, the decisive roll of Gilderoy's thunder. Looking up at the eight feet high Sea Dragons, Cornelia announced, "Game's over. I've got work to do. Time to get on the road to New Hampshire."

"Here, I'll take her place and play a set. The children are fine," Nancy said while picking up a bowling bowl with her long limbs.

Cornelia kissed them good-by and walked across the field to gather her things. As she rode onto the dirt path, she passed Abraham and Sara sorting through the tadpoles in a small, shallow pond. Abraham looked up and waved at her with a light smile. His brightness reassured her and she shouted, "See you later. Love."

Cornelia headed straight for the Eagle's naval academy at Portsmouth. Protected by privateers since the mid-fifteen hundreds, the base supported operations at Annapolis. Having narrowly won the War of 1812, the Eagles considered Annapolis as the spiritual capitol of the struggling nation, especially after the British Hudson Bay company succeeded in burning the White House. Although, Madison remained in office, the president quickly reversed his position and adopted damage-control procedures. Lacking the force to restore the seat of government to Annapolis and pursue the original design of the new nation, the Eagles maintained the compromises established at the Philadelphia conventions. They resigned themselves to the fact that at least, they had established a new nation, which the Eagles, left with little more than a Spirit of 1776, intended to wrangle from the alien-supported commercial enterprises. Things got out of hand when the compromisers shanghied the capitol from Philadelphia, after developing a District of Columbia with Serpentine architects.

"If only the devils had torched Congress's basilica as well," Admiral William Jones roared as he read the documents from Cornelia. "Andrew Jackson whips in the wind to the sound of money. He succeeded in driving the Sicilian mob off the Gulf coast, but handed Dixieland's bank to that shanghai outfit."

"We all wish we were in the land of cotton. We'll have to look in another direction on this on," Cornelia remarked.

Jones glanced at her. The philosophical remarks soothed him. "Isn't someone going to write a song about it? We need something that doesn't follow the tune of *God Save the King*."

Jones offered Cornelia a seat and she sat down at the conference table. Thirty men and women of various shades of skin-color remained silent as they witnessed Jone's response to the news. Jones produced a file for the implementation of the Second Bank of the United States and placed it in front of her. Opening the folder immediately, Cornelia scanned the paperwork. She paged past the notes on external and internal structural design until reaching the section trade agreements.

"I suggest hiding a copy in a secret compartment on one of your ships, Admiral. Put the documents below a red prism, a crystal known as a Vogel."

Leaning back in his chair, Jones commented, "I know just the ship. We put Vogels in most of our vessels. Aubry created them shortly before the American Revolution. This may be part of the reason for our continued success, despite the odds."

Cornelia tucked the papers inside a coat pocket and stayed for the rest of the meeting. Afterward, she met privately with the senior officer at Annapolis. Together, they walked down the main street of the port town. The cold weather kept most of the inhabitants near their hearths. As sleet fell and melted beneath their feet, they stepped cautiously on the cobblestone road, taking it one rock at a time. Tugging on their scarves and hats to wrap the wool tighter over their body, they spoke under breaths that vaporized in the air.

"What do you think of the second bank?"

"We've barely got over the collapse of our first financial institution."

"The problem is the Eye-in-the-Sky and pyramid on the back of the dollar. It's not the bank, but rather the currency, where it goes and what it signifies. We'll never be able to get past that point."

"We aren't looking for a bank to house our money; we are creating ties with the fairy kingdom."

At the end of the block where the gray mists merged with the view of the dark, choppy waves of the sea, the officer hailed the driver of his carriage. He looked around for people who might be watching. Noting the emptiness in the air, he opened the door for Cornelia and she entered. They left the icy white pelts for the frigid booth. Cornelia looked at the ceiling, appearing grateful for the relief from the invasive cold. She smiled at the officer, who also seemed content with the past discourse and mutual understanding.

They travelled to Baltimore, Maryland where a guard ushered them through the back door of the governor's mansion. Cornelia paused a moment to gaze into the night sky. Noting the cloud cover, she lowered her head and focused on her footing along her path. Recognizing the man in uniform, the chief steward ran to them and directed them to a trap door in the floor of the dining room. Cornelia descended the stairs and entered a makeshift cellar. Under the soft glow of candles lining the walls of the sunken room, she embraced her family.

"Mama," a little girl softly cried.

A man with a deep, husky voice added, "We've missed you Cornelia."

"Good to hear," Cornelia responded, blushing slightly as she asserted herself. "Jason, we have work to do."

Five naval officers gathered in the room and listened for the news from Portsmouth.

"It's an SOS," the senior officer revealed. "We want to attract aid from those who sponsored the Anasazi many years ago. They only listen to the fairy kingdom."

Chapter Four

ONE OF THE officers handed Cornelia a Baltimore newspaper. She skimmed the headlines and read an article about the War Hawks in Congress. Though the War of 1812 had ended, the War Hawks persevered, forming a trio which mocked the original three musketeers. Those who had participated in the intricacies of the French Revolution understood the subtle taunt, which amounted to a Roman Triumvirate reminiscent of Napoleon's Sicilian mob. Supported by the same French financiers, the War Hawks pursued world domination, post Rome-style.

Cornelia commented, "The papers have already presented us with William Jones's replacement at the Second National Bank. The War Hawks intend to enslave the entire planet in wars benefitting the Grays."

"Yes, the bank will be short-lived, but it will buy us time to replace the War Hawks in Illinois."

Hearing Jason's simple assessment, the naval officers straightened as his words ran through them and hit the ground. Some blinked as the wheels in their mind fathomed the undertaking. Armed with renewed hope, they immediately left to carry out their new found mission. Shiny tears ran down her cheeks as Cornelia lovingly kissed Jason on his forehead. Gratitude for his enlightened insight beamed through the slight tremble of her upper lip and firm caress of her fingers over his tightly curled dark hair. The ebony hues of their skin melted them into the surrounding darkness. They lingered briefly below the stairs, until the awkward cough of the senior officer stirred them to release their grasp on the other. Jason followed Cornelia out of the room. He bowed at the assembly and left to return to his duties in the kitchen. The little girl took Cornelia's hand. Together they left the mansion for a kitchen in a hotel down the road.

In the bright light of the kitchen, Cornelia rushed to greet familiar faces. After quick hugs and vibrant, moist kisses, they brought Cornelia and her daughter to her quarters. Her suite remained well-hidden among the halls of many, numbered doors. The child fell asleep soon after settling in her bed. Cornelia remained awake, pondering the recent events in the afforded comfort. The relief that came with being reunited with her immediate loved ones cast a different perspective. Sitting down on the end of her bed, she watched the shadows dance on the walls in the flickering light of diminishing beeswax. The forms and distorted shapes reminded her to *mind her beeswax* and focus her awareness on her own business.

"*Mind the bee's wax*," Cornelia murmured to herself as she untangled the stray knots in her hair. Then she laughed as she whispered to her sleeping child, "There is more to life than honey, which is the bee's concern."

She fell asleep beside her. Awaking refreshed, Cornelia busied herself in the kitchen and arranged to visit Dixieland through her network. This time, her daughter, Lacey, travelled with her. When they reached the sacred territory, several Apaches intercepted the wagon caravan and carried them off by horseback. Caught off guard, the settlers failed to put up any defense. The natives left the scene before the wagons circled in formation.

"I'd thought you's never arrive," Cornelia told the band as they entered the orange canyons, far out-of-reach of those questioning her rightful ownership.

"We attempted to send smoke signals, but we didn't want to betray our presence," a warrior said.

Cornelia washed her face in one of the nearby streams as Lacey went off to play with the Native Americans. Making out the rippled form of her features in the water's reflections, she washed away any previous doubt regarding the inherent risks of her mission. The image of the chief wearing his headdress appeared behind hers. She turned around in greeting and rose to acknowledge him.

"We have the Spanish Trail figured out," he communicated through an interpreter. "It is the War Hawks that puzzle us."

"Yes, they have become bloodthirsty," Cornelia admitted. "Calhoun looks like a vampire now."

The chief listened to her interpreted explanation and nodded. Staring at the horizon without blinking, he uttered his response. An interpreter responded, "We saw the same with the Transylvania Land Company and Cherokees."

Jaded by Ponce de Leon's quest for immortality, those subscribing to the cup of Borgia used the ancient Egyptian occultism symbolized on the US dollar to live off the resulting spilled blood. By the time of the congressional triumvirate, the enterprise reached monstrous proportions. Cornelia met with the Apaches for several days. They discussed the Shays Rebellion and developed a business model for reclaiming the Illinois territory. During the Shays Rebellion, refugees from the Battle of Lexington seized the largest armory of the United India Company. They named the town Springfield, in honor of Annapolis's Welsh heritage. The Welsh tied themselves to the planet by assuming last names, which depicted geologic structure. Nancy Hanks husband had masterminded the attack and undermined General Benjamin Lincoln's efforts to shanghai the rest of the population to Asia. Thomas Lincoln served Benjamin Lincoln, a distant relation. After they killed Issac, they sought Nancy as their prisoner, intending to use the family in POW trades with Annapolis. Nancy played their game, fooling her captors in believing that she could be caught. After her spouse passed away, lawyers working with John Marshall fashioned a trust for Issac's children under the legal entity of A. A. Spring. The trust included property, money, and various documents so that the hard-earned victory secured in Springfield, Massachusetts would not perish from this planet.

Cornelia left her daughter under the care of the Apaches, who adopted her as a member of their tribe. After Atlantis fell, aliens invaded and bombed several prominent civilizations in South America. Friendly extraterrestrials carried refugees from the intergalactic port in Peru to a beach, which had been formed by the sand blasted from their former home. In this manner, a new tribe emerged and called themselves Apache. The sand provided them immunity from alien air attacks. The alien's radar systems could not break the spirit that carried the Apaches, who flew over the gulf coastal region on fast, wild mustangs.

Through the league of tribes connected to the Apaches, Cornelia made her way to California. Sneaking into Mission San Gabriel Archangel in the middle of a hot summer day, she witnessed the internment of native populations for silver mining operations. Compared to the other Spanish enterprises, this business surpassed the others in the territory. She covered her face with a shawl and wandered inside the adobe walls. The armed guards ignored her as she feigned a limp and stubbled with the others. Nobody recognized her. When she stood in a room full of people housed side-by-side, Cornelia raised her veil and studied the ceiling. Done with her mission, she exited the next morning the group headed for the local silver mine. Apaches disguised as Mexican raiders rescued her from the ranks of the downtrodden and whisked her away to the desert.

"I only needed to see the ceiling," Cornelia remarked to the chief. "It won't collapse for another century. I can tell you that the war for Mexican Independence will turn out just like the one in New England. The United Mexican States headed by Santa Anna will only hand Napoleon's region over to the United India Company. Santa Anna works with the company patriots, who ultimately serve the Holy Roman Empire."

The chief merely nodded. Her news matched the reports from tribes along the Texas Gulf coast. "The archangel Gabriel has nothing to do with the mission. Michael gave the Native Americans the Aqua de Florida, which Ponce de Leon handed over to British financiers to bottle."

Cornelia stared at the dirt floor of the encampment. "The Aqua de Florida could have been found in many regions on the continent, including Springfield, Massachusetts."

"Jason is correct. With Toussaint gone, we no longer have an opening in South America. We must protect the springs of the sacred waters. Our opportunity lies in the heart of War Hawk country."

"The British companies have been poisoning New England's water supply since the French-Indian Wars."

With those parting words, several Apache warriors escorted Cornelia back to the grocer in St. Louis, who sent supplies and ammunition to Springfield, Massachusetts. Word arrived of the massacre at Elizabethtown in Kentucky. They killed Nancy Hanks and torment all the children. Thomas Lincoln guarded them at his cabin. Meanwhile, the local inhabitants created a story as a cover for the almost twenty people slain by Lincoln's network. The Sea Dragons had vanished, never to return to the area. Shocked by the news, Cornelia sat in a chair near the wood-burning stove in the grocer's office.

"Three years have past since our agents pieced the story together," the head grocer remarked. "Abraham is tongue-tied. He misses his mother greatly and does nothing except read her favorite books. Sara speaks for both of them and cares for Abraham."

Cornelia packed her bags. She told the grocer, "I'll take three sticks of your hard candy. Maybe a little sweetness will loosen Abraham's tongue and he'll tell me what happened. Where's Edward these days?"

"They killed him too, and blamed the Indians. It's another reason why we don't know what happened to the place."

Double J appeared in the doorway. "I overheard your conversation. The Apaches informed me that I could find Cornelia here. Wilkinson's agents claim responsibility for the attacks, but we think that he is serving only as a decoy. Vienna's bankers work behind the scenes. They funded both sides of Napoleon's war with Russia. Now they finance both the Mexican Empire and Santa Ana enterprises."

Cornelia turned toward the grocer, "I will need a white man to escort me to Illinois. I suspect that Thomas Lincoln has taken the children there."

"We have an agent from Annapolis here on the outskirts of town. I'll send for John Shays. His father worked with Issac," the grocer offered.

Within minutes, the agent entered the back of the grocery store. Having already learned of Cornelia's arrival, he decided to shop early. Double J disappeared down the road back to the Gulf coast after providing more details. Cornelia bought four more sticks of candy for the other children that Thomas and his accomplice, named Bush, intended to traffic.

After a brief discussion, John Shays left to gather his belongings and leave his home under the care of a boarder. He met Cornelia on the road to Illinois several miles away from town, where they would not be seen. Together they journeyed to the state capitol at Vandalia, where Queen Charlottte of Sweden placed her vanguard. She died under suspicious circumstances, the same year as Nancy Hanks and the Queen consort of England. The powers seizing Europe and the North American continent swept away the women who made world history. This agenda reflected the rewritten history of the Battle of Lexington, which had been heard around the world because of the women involved.

Reaching Vandalia, Cornelia inquired about the kidnapped children from Kentucky, while John went to the docks on the Kaskaskia River. Noticing the ships marked with the insignia of the skull and bones pirates, John jumped aboard one of the vessels unnoticed. He made his way to the ship's log in the first mate's cabin. Closing the door tightly behind him, John perused the documents. The stamp of the Transylvania Land Company from South Carolina marked the cover of the parchment. Satisfied, he quickly left the ship and met Cornelia in the kitchen of one of the town's hotels. He joined her in the kitchen and slipped her a note. It read: *Calhoun's settlement*. Cornelia slipped behind an open cupboard and glanced at the note. She nodded her agreement at John as he glanced in her direction before shouldering a tray destined for the dining hall.

Chapter Five

"THE WAR HAWKS run the wars to break up families for the human traffickers, which fund the empires," John whispered in the ear of one of the diners.

The seated man quickly nodding his understanding as he heaped mash potatoes on his plate. John served the rest of the guests in the noisy room before leaving with a pile of dirty dishes for the kitchen. There, he found Cornelia taking off her apron and heading outside into the blackness. In the brisk air, Cornelia walked slowly to her horse tied beside John's. She mounted the steed and rode away to secluded hut a mile down the trail.

Two dark-skinned women opened the door to her knock and quickly ushered her inside. Warming herself by the hearth, Cornelia conversed with the head of staff for the small outpost. Removing a mask from his face, the French soldier listened attentively to the story. He responded, "The lynch mobs have started wearing white sheets like the ones in South Carolina. Their horses bear the markings of the newly rebuilt Fort Dearborn, once the site of the Mission of the Guardian Angel."

"Your mask reminds me of my father. He was trained as a musketeer," Cornelia commented in a soft voice. The pensive expression on her face became more pronounced as she added, "The missions off the West coast continue to thrive in the open, while the operations here must be cloaked."

Cornelia rose suddenly and looked through an opening in one of the windows. The moon shone brightly on this clear night. She watched John walk his horse around the yard. After tying him to a bush in the shadows, he hurried to the front door. Cornelia unlocked the door and directed him inside. After a brief discussion, they took turns standing guard while the others slept.

The next evening, John left the hut to find Thomas's whereabouts. He learned about his place in Indiana and took the road, which connected the Indiana location to the former farm in Missouri. Within days, he arrived at Thomas's cabin. Hiding in a nearby grove, he scouted the area for Thomas and his new partner. He saw Abraham chopping wood two hundred yards away. Thomas and his wife worked in a garden on the other side of the house. The other children tended the animals in the barn. Abraham put down his axe and wandered in John's direction. John remained in his position.

"I saw you tie your horse further down the trail," Abraham told him as he came nearer.

"Don't tell anyone that I'm here," John responded. "I knew your mother, Nancy Hanks."

Abraham stepped back and wiped a dry tear from his eye. "I miss her."

"We all do," John said, handing him a stick of candy, one which Cornelia had bought at the grocer. "Did your mama ever mention your daddy?"

"Sara told me," Abraham replied as he thoughtfully rubbed his forehead. "What can I do for you, mister?"

"I brought your guardian, Cornelia Mitchell. She helped your mama deliver you in Alabama."

Abraham sighed and looked down on the ground. "Thanks for the candy." Then he glanced in the direction of the garden where Thomas and his wife plowed. Facing John again, he decided, "Thomas leaves for Indiana in a couple of days. Mrs. Bush goes with him. Soldiers from Fort Dearborn patrol the roads so that we don't runaway. We'd have to swim the river to escape."

"Time to learn how to swim, Abraham."

Abraham grinned. "We can manage."

John placed six sticks of candy in Abraham's palm and closed it firmly. "I worked with your father. He was a good man."

Abraham headed back to the woodpile as John disappeared in the woods. He untied his horse and camped on a secluded hill, where he could watch Thomas and Mrs. Bush. Speaking again with Abraham the next day, John took Abraham by the hand and led him to the river. A boat with three hunters waited for them at the water's edge. Abraham stepped inside the craft and sat down on one of the benches. Taking an oar, he helped the hunters row across the river. At the water's edge, John and Abraham jumped out of the boat and landed on the small sandy beach. Abraham followed John up a steep, rocky hill for the cover of the dense forest. They hiked through the woods until reaching the hut, where Cornelia stayed with the others.

Abraham entered the single room structure and greeted the others in the dim light of the hearth's fire. His eyes met the musketeer's and he smiled. "You're the man, who wears the mask. I've seen you scare away the patrols. They think that you are an Indian."

Cornelia interjected, "He's a musketeer from France, just like my father in Jamaica. Abraham, I saw you the day that you were born. Sara might remember me. Your folks were wonderful people."

"I was lucky that way," he said. Then he added, "I am concerned about the others. If they find that I am gone, then they might get mad and kill them. Thomas gets into rages."

"Put this in his whiskey," Cornelia insisted, handing a tiny bottle to Abraham. "It will put him to sleep and he'll wake up confused."

Abraham quickly pocketed the bottle. "I need to get back before they notice that I'm across the river."

He turned on his heels and closed the door behind him. With a nod in Cornelia's direction, John Shays hurried to catch up with him. The others shrugged at the boy's abrupt departure, while Abraham stepped out into the bright winter day. He stopped to catch his breath several yards away from the hut. The area remained free from sheet-wearing masked marauders. Abraham looked at the glistening, iced dew drops melting in the afternoon sun. The bared trees displayed their plump buds, promising verdant new growth for the next season. Abraham smiled as he sniffed the fresh air. Without waiting for John to speak, he remarked, "The Sea Dragons have handed us our destiny. We can expect no more interference from Gilderoy and Paisley."

John stood beside Abraham and bowed his head to study the youth's stature, which rose to his shoulder. He chuckled slightly, "We knew that their presence was only temporary. They got things moving after Camelon fell and Constantine's Turks sacked Scotland."

Abraham began walking briskly toward the wooded path leading back to the river crossing. He decided, "I feel free for the first time in my life. It tastes as sweet as the candy stick you offered me. Let's go get the others."

"Keep going, while I repack my things and arrange to bring the rest to safety. I'll meet you at the river. The hunters will be looking for you. If I don't arrive, let them ferry you across."

Abraham raced back to the river and found the hunters, who kept watch for John and Cornelia. By the time he reached the river, he saw Cornelia waiting at the bank. Surrounded by chiefs from the Iroquois Confederacy, she towered above the bank from the heights of her horse. As Cornelia watched at him to come closer, several natives readied a canoe to cross the river. Silently they waved him inside the craft and paddled him across. John Shays and the hunters remained absent from this latest twist in his foray. When the natives deposited him on the opposite bank, Abraham cautiously leaped out of the canoe and surveyed the property for signs of Thomas or Mrs. Bush. In the lingering twilight of sundown, he rushed down his beaten path to the river and returned to the cabin. Finding it vacant, he searched the barn for his sister and friends.

Sara emerged from behind one of the cows and wiped her hands her apron before informing Abraham in a low voice. "Thomas and Mrs. Bush left on urgent business. Indians attacked the port at the capitol."

The heads of two other children appeared from the mounds of hay piled against the wall. Wide-eyed, they stared at Abraham. Dennis Hanks, their cousin, quickly began helping the younger children pack for the journey ahead. Almost ten years older than Abraham, he bore a series of whip scars across his chest, which remained hidden from view underneath his buckskin shirt. Without flinching, he gathered the rest of the children and led the procession down to the river's bank. Abraham became the last person in the line, after having altered the scenery to make it look as if natives had seized the youngsters. Hunters armed with rifles met them at the crossing, while the Indians scouted the area and kept watch for intruders. Three boats carried them away to the town of Calhoun in Sangamon County. The settlement served as an outpost for the War Hawks' human trafficking. When his boat docked in Calhoun, Dennis left on the next excursion bound for Oregon. His younger sister, also named Sarah, went with a family bound for Arkansas. She and Abraham had been born the same year, though their mothers birthed the children in different states. Sarah's mother delivered her baby in Tennessee to avoid being tracked by the same bounty hunters compelling her sister, Nancy, to flee to Alabama. Sarah's father had served with Davy Crockett in the county militia. Killed in action during a skirmish with Jackson's hired Indian raiders, Sarah's father left his family several timepieces that communicated with benevolent extraterrestrials. Intervention by the extraterrestrials saved the lives of the children from Wilkinson, an agent representing Spain's interests in the new world. Using the time pieces, Sarah taught Abraham how to sidestep aliens and elude capture by the their representatives on the planet, known as the

Grays. Unfortunately, the protection proved limited as the extraterrestrial ships barely escaped Lucifer's Eye-in-the-Sky aircraft. After having destroyed the intergalactic pentagon, the Eye-in-the-Sky ruled the celestial realms. Anasazi supported the benevolent airships during intergalactic wars plaguing the pyramid civilizations. They entrusted similar timepieces to the Zuni and Cornelia had inherited one from her father, a musketeer.

The geometric designs woven in the tapestries of those inhabiting Dixieland depicted the structure of the intergalactic pentagon, which had been encapsulated in Metatron's Cube. The geometries resonated with portals embedded in Metraton's Cube. In this manner, the survivors restored the intergalactic pentagon, which existed in hologram form. Each piece created became part of the whole. The designs became crystalized in woven blankets, earthenware pots, and watch mechanisms. Lacking coherency in their internal structure, Lucifer's illumined ones failed to track those using the geometric networks. Abraham slipped in the various dimensions for cover and survived, while others fell victim to the traffickers. He lived in a world where a second counted. Timing became everything in eluding capture. These dynamics enabled him to understand his mother from an entirely different perspective, though he failed to understand why it had not work for the attack which took her life.

After Dennis and his sister left, Abraham stayed with the others in Vandalia and drilled with Charlotte's Swiss Guard. The guards hid their identities by adopting the garb of the frontiersmen and pioneer women. The crew, which had rowed Abraham and the others to freedom, consisted of Swiss guards. Thomas Lincoln never came looking for the escaped children and told his supervisors that they had been lost in a fire. His memory remained addled from the drugs ingested with Edward's drinks. Busy with extending their operations into new territories, Wilkinson's agents decided to not pursue the matter. Meanwhile, Abraham ran errands for the local post office and learned the majors paths throughout New England. He took over some of Benjamin Franklin's former delivery routes to New York. No one questioned him when he handed out letters and parcels. Having straddled the upper echelons of both the Eagles and United India company, Franklin's establishments remained an uncontested legacy because it provided cover for the opposing parties. His common-law-wife, Deborah Reed ran covert operations for the Eagles until her untimely passing before the American Revolution officially began. Then one lie led to another and compromises obscured the truth about the revolution, which shackled the new nation's inhabitants to the same gangster's funding Napoleon.

The local Vandalia newspapers focused attention on the activities underneath the dome of the basilica in the District of Columbia. Abraham read the papers just enough to converse with the recipients of the letters traversing the continent. People trusted those who consistently delivered communications through wars and weather. He read his mother's books, which had been salvaged by a friendly tribe of Choctaws. As more and more native tribes became interned in public education camps in the Southwest, Cornelia and the Swiss Guard laced the leaders in the general population. Settlements sprang up overnight in some areas. If the Swiss Guards could give up their colorful uniforms for the earthy garb of frontier personnel, then the natives with the more even tempers could follow suit. The astute warriors declined their roles as moving targets and victims. They joining the ranks of Caucasian refugees fleeing the European persecutions on US terrain.

Dennis Hanks continued to refer to his kidnapping by Thomas Lincoln as time spent at *Uncle Tom's Cabin*. He scouted Oregon and wrote letters about the operations of the Hudson Bay Company, which fed the Spanish missions with children. Disguised as Indians, the soldiers killed targeted settlers and rounded up the surviving youngsters like sheep. Cornelia, aware of the circumstances leading to the murder of Meriwether Lewis, ran interference for Dennis. She met with Lyman Beecher, who resumed the work of the Ducks. Led by Nathan Hale, the Ducks represented those opposing the Greek organizations brainwashing students at Yale. After the hanging of John Andre and pursuit of Admiral Rogers of the Queen's Rangers, the Ducks hid the documents developed by the Eagles for the American Revolution. Then they went underground and raised the next generation to carry on their work with the designers of the freedom, which took the lives of their forebears. While the New England newspapers focused on the African slavery issue, Beecher began formally educating females and giving them a voice. Nathan Hale loved the woman, who raised his son by the daughter of the British governor. After the British governor killed her during the confrontation in Lexington, Nathan regrouped with the rest of the Ducks as the patriots betrayed the revolution. Adhering to the biased agenda of the United India company, occultists such as Revere conspicuously erased women from history. Without a voice, females and

Africans continued to be disempowered targets for human trafficking.

Cornelia supplied Beecher with books for his studies and assisted with settling African refugees in Ohio, which offered protection from the turbulence fueled by the French Revolution. Meanwhile the United India company restored Unitarianism in the ranks of the faithful wishing for abstinence from the fervor or rituals plaguing Constantine's version of the Roman Empire. Illegal land transactions pushed the original Mayflower settlements into intern camps. Unitarians replaced the Puritans. Those running the shanghias sought purification through Asian transcendence rituals. They whitewashed the Eastern traditions to counter those seeking reforms. The distortion of the truth created splits in the consciousness. Federalists and Whigs split into Republicans. Puritans split into Church of England and Unitarians. Unitarians split into Baptists, Calvinists, Presbyterians, and Transcendentalists. The polarized Transcendentalists paved the way for a civil war. When the Presbyterians suffered an internal split, Cornelia and Lyman seized the opportunity to move the underground into the political arena. Planting a Presbyterian congregation near the White House, the church served as a haven for those avoiding the trafficking. Caught in their own lies, the United India company patriots used intrigue to accomplish their aims. They could not openly confront those demanding freedom without accounting for the discrepancies. This dynamic brought the Eagles time. Cornelia, like Sarah and the timepieces, instructed Abraham in the value of having time on one's side.

Chapter Six

2003

Ozark Mountains, Arkansas

"HOW DO YOU know?" Joe questioned Tobias as they hiked up the side of Iron Mountain. A bead of perspiration dripped from his short, dark brown hair. Pulling a handkerchief from his pocket, he mopped his brow as he stopped to catch his breath. "Carrie said that the fighting phenomenologists at a university in Dallas convinced themselves that a philosopher could never know anything."

Carrie, the astrophysicist studying the Milky Way at a university observatory, had accompanied Joe on his trek to California. Joined by an osteopath and geologist, they unravelled the intergalactic history of Mexican-American War. Having left a university in Dallas under duress, she learned how to feign ignorance.

Tying her long, dark hair in a ponytail, Michelle, Tobias's wife, quipped, "They named a party after that."

Surveying the valley below them, Tobias fathomed the series of events which had led them to this perspective. Standing taller than those around him, Tobias steadied himself on the slope and took a breath of fresh air, "Oh, yes, the famous Know Nothing Party of the pre-Civil War days."

Michelle worked as a naturopathic midwife, serving a clinic group in Springfield, Oregon. Tobias met her while teaching at a college in Portland. Joe ran into Tobias during a kayak trip in the Pacific Northwest. Lucky for Joe, Tobias came equipped with natural therapies for first aid. He saved Joe from paddling to the closest emergency room with a bleeding hand. After that interlude, the two men become lifelong friends, continuing to protect each other on their journeys.

Glancing askew at Joe, who wore a smirk on his face, Tobias asked, "Now how many margaritas does it take for understanding that?"

Ignoring the jest, Michelle stopped at the edge of a precipice and pointed. "There's the base the station for the spaceships." Turning to Joe, she stated, "There's is a long forgotten method of scientific inquiry existing on its own, outside of the British scientific method developed for the Know Nothings. Preschoolers learn how to connect the dots. The resulting image differs from a Rorschach-ink blot."

"Carrie prefers the development of intact neural networks, as opposed to the sclerotic dead ends characteristic of post War World II Alzheimer's disease," Michelle observed, casually making her way to the base station.

A middle-age, clean-shaven man stood near a small, hut-like structure made out of granite. He waved at her as she approached and greeted, "Hi, Michelle, how are the youngsters in Springfield?"

She hugged him and entered the stone cottage. Both Tobias and Joe hurried on the trail to catch up. When they reached the site where Michelle met the gentlemen, they paused to study the base's use of technology. Several airships stood docked inside the mountain's portal. Michelle's face appeared from the doorway. She playfully tugged at Tobias's shirt and drew him inside the building. Smiling at him and Joe, she told them, "Watch out for departing ships. There's a heavy intergalactic war going on."

"She's wearing the same chagrin as she did yesterday," Joe remarked to Tobias.

"Runs in the Linkhorn family," Tobias mentioned.

"Do you mean Lincoln?" Joe questioned as he examined a control panel next to the gentleman.

His eyes shining, the man listened thoughtfully. Offering Joe a handshake before his fingers touched the panel, he said, "The name is Abraham Linkhorn, I am from the former president's paternal side of the family. He married a Basque, the niece of a gypsy queen fighting for the French during the Sicilian mob's invasion. She became his first wife."

Joe grimaced when he heard his personal account of history. Hesitating to change the subject, he cooly pursued, "Oh, do you mean the French Revolution?"

Abraham give quick, direct single nod as he resumed focus on Joe's activity. Then he moved to Joe's side and stood between him and the instrumentation, "I hear that you are an electronics engineer with part ownership in a California startup company."

Taken aback, Joe pulled away from the board and noted a large crystal in the corner of the office. Eyeing Abraham, he asked, "Who told you that? We came here on a hunch."

"You came here on a hunch. Michelle's Springfield relations retain astral communications with us."

Michelle stared at Joe. "I came here because I knew better."

Tobias glanced at Joe and imitated Groucho Marx with an imaginary cigar and tonal inflection, "It's better than Knowing Nothing."

Failing to amuse Joe, Tobias grabbed Michelle's hand and followed her down bronze staircase. Joe remained standing in the room and collected his wit. Abraham rolled a bronze cover over the panel. After locking the device with a pyramid pointed crystal from his pocket, he left Joe and joined the couple hallway below.

Stepping back outside, Joe saw that the entrance to the opening had been cloaked, presenting the illusion of a typical mountain face. With a sigh, he dove back inside the granite cottage and quietly descended the stairs. At the bottom, he found Michelle, Abraham, and Tobias waiting for him.

Tobias nodded and the group walked down the hall together. Streaming through crevices in the sides of the underground passage, natural lighting illuminated the shiny bedrock floor of the cavern. Crystals of smoky quartz and feldspar glittered in the rays of the setting sun. At the end of the cave, a large room appeared from a shielded entrance of a rock wall. Several people rose from a wooden oak table and shook hands with the newcomers. A collection of guitars, mandolins, bases, and violins dotted the room, lending a cozy air to the stone enclosure.

A tall, lanky gentleman, who introduced himself as Garret Lynch, saw Michelle longingly survey the castanets on a small table filled with percussion instruments. He picked up a pair and clicked the objects swiftly between his palms before offering them to Michelle to play. After a few light clicks, she returned the castanets to their stand as she lifted her head with a transfixed gaze. Every sinew in her body remained alert and aware of the dynamics currents in the surrounding atmosphere.

Tobias approached a guitar resting against the wall. Gesturing at Lynch, he politely asked, "May I?"

Lynch consented and Tobias removed the guitar from its place for a few gentle strums. The fine notes from his fingers touched him and his body relaxed. In a low voice, he sang with feel of the instrument cradled in his arms. "...heard the owl calling my name...we are bound to love...love...love's the word...that's the message heard...we are bound to love...."

People quieted with his initial lines, before becoming inspired and breaking out in hearty chatter. Tobias stood alone, huddle over the guitar to hear every beat that resonated with the vibrations of his heart. Michelle joined Lynch in a lively discussion, while Abraham entertained Joe with more technical gimmicks. Joe deliberately stepped away from Abraham. He sensed Abraham's detached amusement and sought the throng gathered around the table for the big picture view. Pausing briefly as Tobias's background music struck a chord in him, he stopped in his tracks and withdrew his approach. Instead, his eyes glistened with contained tears while he drifted into his own perspective. Tobias put down the guitar and walked over to the huddle at the table.

One of the men looked up from a drawing of the connection between Iron Mountain and Mount Cyllene near Arcadia, Greece. "There's something I want to show you."

Michelle dropped her conversation with Lynch and followed Tobias and the man back into the passageway. A few steps behind, Joe ignored the others in the room and exited with them. Climbing the stairs, they entered the office and headed for the porch. The man peered out a window and cracked the door open to show them the creature sleeping on the deck.

The men froze in their tracks. Michelle grabbed a straw broom tucked in a corner beside the desk and whisked it through the opening. "It's just Bob the cat."

"It's a large bobcat," Joe commented, his eyes wide. "They don't slumber on my porch in California."

"Shoo," Michelle said as she brushed the animal away.

With a decisive air, the mountain lion scampered off into the brush, seeming pleased that he had been noticed.

"Ah Michelle, you brought us another totem," Tobias said as the others joined him and Michelle on the granite steps outside. "It's time to walk the talk."

The man offered Joe an astonished sideways glance before leading down a tunnel near the station. After submerging three hundred yards into the earth's interior, they entered another cavern. A sheet of translucent mica lined the far end, allowing an observer to gain a perspective on the MidEarth.

Having trailed them down the tunnel, Abraham entered the silence of the cavern as he offered cryptically, "Don't bother chronicling Narnia."

Tobias blinked with the shock of recognition. The MidEarth resembled a pre-exploded mine field. The devastation appeared so severe that a darkness hung over the land like a nuclear plume. He looked toward the exit.

"Got it," he said moving away from the scene.

Michelle drew Tobias's attention toward a familiar shape hovering over a pile of rubble. "It's Bilbo the hauflin."

This is what I wanted to show you," Bilbo communicated. Though his stature remained light and bright with his news commentator pose, a steel rod seemingly ran through his constitution, grounding him firmly in terra firma. Finding strength in the confrontation with the reality, he sorted through the debris, bringing hope to whatever he salvaged. *"You must join me to obtain the information on Iron Mountain."*

The man, who had showed them the portal to the MidEarth, took them through another series of passageways until they found themselves on the other side of the mica sheet. Bilbo waved the man off and he went to rejoin Abraham, who continued to watch from the mica window on the devastated shire. Bilbo led them to a small, makeshift hut, which he had restored as part of his original dwelling. Inside, the structure appeared much larger than its outward image.

Bilbo explained, "Like Iron Mountain, I use principle of optics to create a smaller real image. The trick is to invert the upside image, which serves as my cover. I can refract and play with the daylight like a fairy."

He offered them a small feast at the dining table. In contrast to the destruction outdoors, his humble abode seem warm and cozy. As he filled their bowls with stew and passed them around the table, he aded, "After we sent the fairies to help with the American Revolution, I secured my private space."

As they partook of the fare, Bilbo left them briefly to retrieve a thick book from his library, situated in an alcove neat the hearth. He placed the heavy book on the table with a thud. Opening to the first page, he read the title, *"Pre-Eden Origins of Iron Mountain, Volume One."*

Michelle paused before taking the next spoonful. "Friends tell us that the exposed rock is at least five-hundred million-years-old. Some places beneath the surface could be as much as two-thousand six hundred-million years old, almost half of the earth's age."

Joe gulped and put his utensil aside. He added more hot water to his cup of tea as he sat back and reflected on the passage of time. Tobias continued eating, not missing a beat in his famished state.

"You should hear about the other half of the earth's history," Bilbo quipped. "There's been many transformations through the ages."

Bilbo slammed the book shut and left it resting on the table. Michelle pushed her dishes to the side and reached for the volume. Tobias stopped for a moment, looking over her shoulder as she turned the pages. Brightly colored illustrations flooded the divisions between pages of script, written in American.

"The volumes speak to the dialect of the reader, which in your case is American. If I were to read the note, I might relate to the subject matter in terms of old English."

Tobias looked up in amazement at the fluidity of communication. "Hooray for technology."

"Some of the best tools are ancient," Bilbo remarked. "Why reinvent the wheel?"

"Communication must have been import to the origins of these notes," Michelle commented. Rising from her chair, she stated, "Excuse me, I have a little light reading to do by the fire."

As she cleared her place and washed her dishes, Tobias scanned the text before she returned for it. Hurriedly, he deciphered the contents in contrast to the pictures, a technique he cultivated for absorbing large amounts of information quickly. When Michelle came the book, he glanced at her with a smile as she took it away to read in a soft chair.

Baffled by Tobias's reaction to the book, he leaned across the table. "So what did the book on Iron Mountain say."

Bilbo left to clean his kitchen. Tobias looked around, making sure that Michelle could not overhear him. Adjusting his voice, he provided his private opinion, "A group of hostages from other places in the universe were held on the planet by the nephilim. Using the passage of time, they overthrew their captors and learned how to live with the rhythms of the planet, which eventually proved hostile to their oppressors. In fact, the hostages became so clever that they learned how to incorporate their desire for light and freedom into the earth's structure, creating changes supporting life."

Joe sat back in his chair and ran his fingers threw his short dark hair. "It's a plan."

"This volume documents the changes they mades, so that they could keep track and seed hope in other realms."

With eyes half-closed, Michelle closed the book softly and reclined in her seat. "I heard that."

Tobias grinned at Joe, who smiled back at him. Tobias said in a loud voice, "It is like the sponge, one of the most primitive organisms known in the biological hierarchy of complexities. The simple sponge emits an odor to keep predators away."

Joe crossed his arms with his forearms flat on the table. Looking at Tobias as if he was striking a deal, he said, "So, if the planet stinks, predators leave us alone?"

Tobias reclined in his chair. "It's all relative."

Refreshed, Michelle rose from chair and joined the discussion in the dining area. Putting one hand on Tobias's should as she stood near, she remarked, "Okay, you masked men, what do we do next?"

"Wear masks, for one," Tobias rejoined. "Seize the opportunity in chaos and take advantage of the planet's being in an overextended state."

Without a word, Bilbo sat down at the table. He asked them, "So what are you going to do about the werewolves?"

"Werewolves?" Joe questioned. "Where do they come from?"

"Werewolves keep the planet in its overextended state and threaten life on Iron Mountain." Taking a deep breath, Bilbo explained the origins of werewolves. "Lycaon became the first werewolf."

"Oh, I remember the Greek myth," Michelle said as she sat down. "It is another story of the constellations. It has to do with the naming of Ursa major and Ursa minor. Ursa means bear."

"Iron Mountain has a connection to Mount Cyllene, the birthplace of the swift-footed god, Mercury. Mercury served as a messenger and gave earth Metatron's Cube, which contains information from the intergalactic pentagon."

Chapter Seven

"I WORKED WITH Metatron's Cube during my undergraduate studies," Tobias said.

"Tobias and Joe mask their concern with humor," Michelle confessed for the two.

Bilbo nodded, gazing thoughtfully at those seated around him. "It is time that you head back. You don't want to overdo it. The book stays here. Come again when you need to borrow it."

Tobias rose from the table and cleared his place. Joe carried his plate in the kitchen behind his friend and together they quickly cleaned up after themselves. As Joe finished hand-drying the last dish, he mentioned, "You must tell me about Ursa major and minor when we get back."

Bilbo grabbed several pairs of glasses with horse blinders before escorting them back to the passageway. "Here, wear these so that the rest of the devastation remains hidden from your view. It's been very traumatic, so you must keep looking forward."

Tobias quickly donned a pair and left the hut for the tiny path through the debris. The others followed Tobias with Bilbo bringing up the rear. The left the glasses with Bilbo and thanked him for his consideration. By the time they reached the mica window, a group of men and women from the station ushered them through the tunnels without a second glance. They arrived at the opening past the conference room by nightfall.

Under the starry sky, they peered into the darkness for the sight of familiar vegetation and collected their wit. Tobias eyed Michelle, "Do you want to spend the night here? Joe and I can manage without you in the cabin."

Abraham offered to give the two men a lift back into town. He kept his jeep parked on the other side of the office and drove the back roads into town. Tobias and Joe walked with Abraham to the vehicle, while Lynch accompanied Michelle to the guest suite where she could continue talking with her relations.

During the trip down Iron Mountain, Joe encouraged Abraham and Tobias to tell him the story of Ursa major and minor. Abraham nodded in consent and began his version of the story. Tobias remained silent and watched the dark shadows leap by them as the moonlight danced through trees they passed.

When the earth was only ten thousand years old, aliens from other universes attacked Arcadia. Arcadia initially existed as star system twenty-two dimensions away. A handful of survivors came to this solar system to help defend it from upcoming invasions. The hostages overthrew their captors and created Iron Mountain and other communication stations such as the Matterhorn in Europe. During that the time, a large ocean covered most of the planet, these mountains appeared on the surface as island.

Some of the sponsors of the refugees went to the dark side and failed to incarnate on the planet. Enlightened beings from a star system sixty dimensions away gave the inhabitants on Iron Mountain almost a dozen Titans as a gift. The leader of the star system was called Aether. Each Titan personified a spiritual attribute and could be titrated against the antimatter left behind by their former captors. They brought the Titans to a laboratory outpost at present day Mount Othrys, Greece. One of the Titans, called Rhea, flowed well with the violent time entity known as Cronus. After an attack by the Serpentines, the time entity began eating its young. Rhea went with the flow and successfully hid one of the offshoots, who bore the name Zeus. Zeus discarded Cronus and formed a new establishment on a cloud hovering over Mount Olympus, though the entity could only master the form of an eagle on the planet. Zeus's cloud sabotaged the refugee operations from Andromeda, a cooperative of ascended artisans.

The huntress Diana managed the human form and protected the nymphs housed at Mount Cyllene. The nymphs cultivated the earth's spirit after Zeus's cloud finished off Eden after the Serpentines penetrated the minds of the inhabitants. With Lilith's assistance, the Serpentines developed counter prototypes to the human forms in Eden. Pelagus, Lilith's son with Lucifer, mimicked Adam in many aspects, though he sidestepped complications and mated with an ocean nymph. To clear the cloud dominating the planet, Iron Mountain developed a human life form, which personified Zeus. Zeus II assumed Diana's prototype and impregnated one of the huntress' nymphs called Callisto. Like the rest of the nymphs, Callisto exercised free choice and will. Choosing to go to the light, Callisto sought refuge from Pelagus, the Serpentine version of a human male.

Meanwhile Callisto's father, Lycaon, tested Zeus II to determine weak points for the Serpentines to exploit. Callisto hid her son, Arkas, in Arcadia as Serpentines gained control of the entity known as Hera. Like her sibling Cronus, Hera threatened to eat the young of Zeus II. The nymph Callisto assumed the form of a bear and hid in a cave. The nonhuman form made her imperceptible to the radar of the Serpentines.

As refugees from the universe began working with Iron Mountain, Persephone provided the two Kings of the Pleiades with seven nymphs. After the fall of Eden, a new infrastructure was needed for the transport of souls between the heaven and earth. The Pleiades proved to be the most immune from the Serpentine attacks and served as the godhead. Their divinity served those managing the refugees through the Orion Council. The eldest nymph, Maia, weaved the web of illusion representing the essence of being and devised the Mayan calendar, ending the deal with the Serpentines in 2012. She raised Arkas in a cave on Mount Cyllene, near the place where Persephone had birthed her. Working with Prometheus, Arkas brought heaven to earth and taught artisan forms of basket weaving and baking bread. Their work helped secure a site for the refugees from Andromeda.

Lycaon attacked Arkas and threatened to torture him in the same manner that Zeus I bound and tortured Prometheus. Due to his training as hunter, Arkas understood the nature of Serpentine hybrids and those personifications unwilling to make a choice. He appealed to Zeus II for help. Enlisting the aid of the Thunder People, Zeus II saved Arkas and destroyed all witnesses to his son's torture. Those who watched made a passive choice to side with the Serpentine agenda. The Thunder People torched Lycaon's house with a single stroke of lightning. Permanently reduced to his impaired male domestic instincts, Lycaon became a werewolf. Like Zeus I, the only form that he could assume on the earth plane was mad wolf, resembling his great-grandfather Lucifer. The werewolf began a cult for Zeus I that demanded human sacrifice. In this manner, the Serpentines intended to regain their form and displace the original human prototype.

Both Arkas and his mother, Callisto, ascended to the heavens to avoid the mayhem. They sponsored another group of refugees on the planet, which later became known as the Arctos, or Bear clan. Free from deity homage in the Diana model, these refugees learned how to escape persecution by living in the northern caves. The caves circled around the protective eye of those inhabiting Ursa major and Ursa minor.

Abraham concluded his story and pointed out the Bear constellations when he stopped in front of the cabin. Reaching inside his wallet, he pulled out a dollar bill. He shone his flashlight on the green border of the note.

"See, here is Hera's owl hidden in the subtle design."

Tobias shivered. "Let's get inside where it's warm. I want to take a better look."

Joe unlocked the door to the cabin and flipped on the lights. Tobias removed a bill from his wallet and studied it underneath a lamp. Joe looked over his shoulder at the owl's image.

"*I heard the owl call my name*," Abraham repeated to Tobias.

"According to Native Americans living in the Pacific Northwest, the call of an owl is an ominous sign. It signals the end of a person's life." Tobias handed the note to Joe and shook his head. "The metaphor applies to the tribe itself, as well as the inhabitants of our planet."

"That's the big picture," Joe added with a nod. He gave the bill back to Tobias. who put it away in his wallet.

"Now we know that the caller is the work of Hera," Tobias said. "The natives used myth to explain the world ASIS, as opposed to ISIS, which reconfigures the earth's fragments in her own image---not pretty."

"There's a lot to be said for sanity," Joe said with a blink. He put his hands on his hips as if to block any tempering of his mental functions. Standing firm in his position, he appeared as a mountain of iron.

Abraham stared at the two men. "Nobody is called to death on Iron Mountain. We are bound for glory but not glory-bound."

"We are here for our freedom," Joe asserted. "Like the inhabitants on Iron Mountain."

"It's a deal," Abraham told Joe. "Ever since Gondwanaland, the earth's resources have been exploited to serve the Serpentine's agenda. Our money literally goes to outer space or some cloud in the sky."

"Some presidents have attempted to wrestle the dollar away from Greek deities," Tobias commented.

Abraham said in a soft voice, "They incur the wrath of the gods from alien ships and their materialistic minions." He turned and headed for his jeep parked outside. Closing the door behind him, he offered, "Come to Iron Mountain tomorrow and we can discuss this further. Good night."

Joe and Tobias made a trip to a nearby city for more supplies and hiked up the mountain afterwards. Passing by the site where Michelle had spotted the base station, they failed to find their way back. After several hours, they returned to the cabin. Joe placed his pack down on the floor and pulled a dollar from his wallet. He studied the image of the owl.

"I think that if we learn how to see this owl, then we'll be able to reach Michelle," he told Tobias.

With an air of determination, Tobias refilled his water bottle before shouldering his pack. Joe followed him on the trail. When they reached the site where they had spotted the base station, Joe pointed to a bird flying overhead. Tobias whipped out his binoculars and identified the rapture as falcon. They tracked the falcon's flight to a grove of trees twenty feet away. Nearing the alders, Tobias saw the base station appear over the horizon. Making their way through dense underbrush, the men forged a new path as they recalled how easy their journey had been with Michelle.

They stopped at the stone cottage and caught their breath. Michelle waved at them from the heights of a distant platform towering over them. Joe took a deep breath and eyed Tobias with an air of resignation.

Michelle cupped her hands over her mouth and shouted, "What took you so long?"

"We got lost," Tobias screamed over the mountain top. He grinned and shrugged his response at Joe.

"That's odd," Michelle replied. Without saying anything further, she turned and climbed down a ladder.

Tobias and Joe sat down on a rock and waited for Michelle to join them. Within minutes she appeared on the ledge and rushed to hug and kiss Tobias. Grasping Joe's hand in hers, she squeezed it lightly. "I'm happy that I decided to spend the night. We might not have been able to find this place again."

Abraham emerged from the stone office and shook hands with the two men. "Welcome back."

Tobias looked at the falcon soaring overheard. Turning toward Michelle, he said in a serious, low voice, "We are given life as mystery without a text or road map."

Joe nodded. "A good deed opens up a portal, which reflects the blessings and miracles in our lives. a lawyer and an artist friend, told me this once."

The group entered the office and descended the stairs leading to the mica window. Tobias peered through the translucent glass into the MidEarth. The others grimaced when they reviewed the devastation. A curl of smoke danced in a light wind above Bilbo's quiet hut. Bilbo did not appear in the scene. After a moment of reflection, Tobias broke the silence, "How about going back to the conference room and regrouping?"

Abraham nodded and ushered them back through the tunnel. Inside the conference room, Tobias sat down at the table with the rest. He told those gathered around him about a trip that he and Joe took to Fort Smith last night. "We caught the early morning tour of the museum. Joe and I were surprised to learn that the job of a US Marshal was to recover runaway slaves."

"Eventually the area became a haven for runaway slaves, orphans, and Southern Unionists, and victims of the guerrilla warfare on both sides," one man explained. "Descendants of those who fought in the Battle of Lexington moved in to protect Iron Mountain. They came and helped with operations. They kept the marauders from the Dallas settlement from taking over Oklahoma with their bots."

"Bots," Michelle whispered. Bots referred to the humans. who had chosen to collude with the robotics of an alien agenda.

"The Dallas settlement controlled the large ranches in Southeast Texas. Compared to the Persian influence on the development of the US Pentagon, the Dallas operation proved to be just a sideshow. The five-pointed structure relates to the British-Iranian discovery in the Mideast."

"What did they find?" Michelle asked.

"The Epic of Gilgamesh fueled the Mexican-American War," a woman answered. Sitting across from Tobias, she folded her arms across her chest with a sigh. "The cult of Dionysus, the Civil War incarnation of the League of Shadows, wanted to extend the alien base headquartered at a chateau in France."

Tobias sat back in his chair. A sense of overwhelm flooded his countenance. "What do we do now?"

"Stay centered like being in the middle of well-balance bicycle wheel and invoke the Serenity Prayer used in Assisi, Italy," Abraham said.

"Substitute an *a* for an *i* and word becomes assassins," Tobias noted. He stared hard at those gathered at the table. "The Serenity Prayer affirms the fact that some aspects of reality must be accepted."

Abraham clasped his hand together and rested his forearms on the table. He met Tobias's gaze and politely reminded him, "Narnia is only an hour's drive from Assisi. C. S. Lewis claimed that he chose the town because it was halfway to Rome."

Pulling a book out on the subject, Abraham opened the pages to the chapter on Narnia and slid the volume across the table to Tobias. Tobias accepted the book and skimmed the contents. According to the volume, when the Romans seized the region from a tribe of Atlantean survivors, they practiced psychological warfare and renamed the town. Narnia meant worthlessness.

Tobias looked up from the pages. "So there is nothing to chronicle. It is all worthless."

"Correct," Abraham replied. "Nothing for the Romans to write home about, even if they lived in Britain."

Michelle looked up from the table and commented, "Only someone like Gilgamesh would consider the survivors of a flood as worthless. What one values, one sees."

Abraham interrupted Tobias's reading and turned the pages to a chapter at the end of the book. Entitled *EUR*, the text provide the context for the chronicles. Narni surfaced as a planned community destined for the site of a world exposition. The acronym *EUR* translated to Rome's exposition on the Universe, which promoted Mussolini's fascist designs. After World War II, the community reorganized in Switzerland and assumed the name Permanent Industrial Exposition. By 1958, many of the war-related industries had achieved solidarity. A subsidy of Permanent Industrial Exposition created an International Trade Mart in New Orleans. The company behind the trade marts bore the name Centro Mondiale Commeriale, the Italian translation for *World Trade Center*. The New Orlean's operation enjoyed protection from the organization established by the grandson of Napoleon III. This organization became known as the Federal Bureau of Investigation. During the French Revolution, a Greek artist named Rigas Feraios brought the French Revolution to the Balkans and transformed the enterprise into a religious war, characteristic of the Crusades of the Dark Ages. Using the name Constantine Rigas, the protege from Mount Olympus found support at a monastery on the remote Mount Pathos. His actions can only be understood by Danny Casolaro's twenty-first century description of the Octopus. Vienna, Napoleon's common base with Rigas and the Hapsberg Empire, and Constantinople, the Pentarchy held by the Turks rather than the Ottomans, represented two arms of the Octopus. The head of the Octopus remained with the Orion Council, which had been infiltrated by the Eye-in-the-Sky near the time of the collapse of the intergalactic pentagon. Lucifer's minions kept an eye on world trade. All investments benefitted the outfit in outer space and robbed the planet of its spiritual value. With designs on world currency, the Eye-in-the-Sky capped the pyramids of economy.

Choices from the American Revolution

The head of alien affairs during World War II eventually replaced Napoleon III's grandson as head of the Federal Bureau of Investigation. The Balkan Federation proved instrumental in the president's assassination in Dallas. The president died on the way to the Dallas World Trade Mart, a sizable outpost on the Silk Road encompassing the globe by the American Revolution. An informant for the Federal Bureau of Investigation testified that Carlos Mantello admitted running the assassination. The US government released the information from the National Archives in 2006. As part of the French heroin network, Mantello received orders from a *big fish* in the Chicago outfit, while doing a run near Halifax, Nova Scotia. Those masterminding the coverup for the American Revolution made Halifax their headquarters. The order for the assassination came from the richest family of the United India company in New England. A descendant confessed to having "snooped" during the Kennedy administration and ordered the hit without consulting his company of pirates. The book entitled *Closet Red: A Marxist's Adventure Inside the Ruling Class* equated the operation to an African safari. The US Pentagon sufficed for the scavenging jackal in this case. Those working the French heroin network wanted to prevent the US Pentagon from intervening in the case for Algerian independence, which would have decreased company revenue. Along with Franco Spain, Gladio (an Italian terrorist organization), and the Organization of the Secret Army (representing Algeria), the infiltration of the intergalactic haven for refugees no longer existed. The persecutors had taken the Orion Council for their own purposes and pursued the refugees for Lucifer.

Chapter Eight

JOE TOOK A dollar bill from his wallet. With his right index finger, he outlined the image of Hera's owl in the green border. He traced the uncapped pyramid with his finger. Joe remarked, "It seems strange that those seeking independence on this continent would invoke an image from ancient Egypt. Sorta makes those using the currency think that the God of their nation lives in another country."

"It's a decoy," Tobias said, rising from the table. "The cabal running the United States inhabits Narnia. I want to see Bilbo again."

He left the room and Joe followed without saying a further word. Michelle remained at the table with the others. Her hands wiped a tear from the corner of her eye as she mentioned, "I don't want to see that place again, not in its present condition. I want to move forward. Let Tobias go. Joe can help him deal."

The meeting ended as quickly as it began. Michelle went outside with the others for a breath of fresh air. Meanwhile, Tobias and Joe made their way through the underground cavities to the Mid-Earth.

Bilbo waited for them at the entrance with pairs of green glasses. "I heard that you were coming. I've developed these for now. They filter out the devastation and color everything green. Let's go."

They made their way to Bilbo's hut and removed the spectacle. Tobias peered at the cozy, warm furnishings. Joe took a deep breath after removing his glasses.

"Tell me about Narnia," Tobias began as Bilbo ushered the two men to join him at the table.

In anticipation of their arrival, Bilbo had spread a light feast. He lit a candle and filled their cups with hot, mulled cider. Handing a cup to Joe, he explained, "The cult of Dionysus instructed Benjamin Franklin's first wife to infuse the currency with the occult symbols. They were having a good time and didn't want the party to end. You need money for parties, especially political ones." Helping himself to a hearty bowl of stew, he added, "The cabal in Narnia controlled the world, while the Romans partied in Rome. Another cabal in Armenia put in their two cents, so to speak."

Tobias rose and found a book in Bilbo's library on the subject. Helping himself to the text, he browsed through the contents and found the chapter on Narnia. Bilbo did not interrupt him. Instead, he glanced about his humble abode, grateful for the potential assistance in cleaning up the mess outdoors. Meanwhile, Tobias ignored Joe and Bilbo's light chatter as he studied the design of Narnia's coat of arms. The image depicted a red nephilim.

Sensing Tobias's next question, Bilbo interjected in a loader voice, "The Civil War became a battle to protect the MidEarth and the base at Iron Mountain. The MidEarth suffered enormous devastation, but survived."

Tobias closed the book and joined Joe and the hauflin at the table. Sipping his cup of mulled cider, he reflected on the latest information, Turning to Bilbo, he said, "Let me guess, "Edgar Allan Poe served as triple agent."

"Linkhorn didn't mention it?" Bilbo queried, setting down his biscuit as he munched on a turkey leg.

"No, we haven't got that far," Joe mentioned with the slight air of a comic, who played it straight.

"He met with Lafayette during his visit to America. Lafayette called his father, David Poe, Jr., the *General.* He filled the spot left by the triple agent, John Andre. Both men used poems to convey top secret information concerning Annapolis, the original capital of the America Revolution."

Joe nodded at Tobias and looked at his watch. Bilbo noticed the nonverbal interaction and retrieved a small book from his alcove. Handing it over to Tobias, he told him, "There's one more piece to the story. As a poet, Poe knew the political theater. Dion Boucicault played the lead role in the *Vampire. Uncle Tom's Cabin* hit the theaters that year, along with some of Alexander's Dumas plays. Forced to flee France as the *Vampire* played in America, Dumas became famous for his stories on the musketeers."

Tobias stood and quickly thumbed through the pages. A caption below a photograph of Boucicault described his association with the Chateau Germaine, the palace in France with the famed alien statue centered in grounds. His theater cult sponsored Dion Fortune's enterprises in England during World War II. Her evening parties included many high ranking world leaders. Naval Intelligence sent agents to Dion's parties, where they began to uncover the link with the Lincoln assassination. Boucicault worked with Ford, who operated theaters and invested in railroad companies.

Tobias continued skimming the text. James Madison's Secretary of War established the ranches in southeast Texas. One of the marshals named for the Dallas settlement married the daughter related to the ranch and Secretary of War. Other ranching relations mistakenly killed Anthony Wayne, a war hero, and instigated the Newburgh conspiracy that tarnished George Washington's reputation. The older brother of Madison's Secretary of War practiced with Dr, Benjamin Rush. A student of Dr. Rush's bled Washington to death.

Turning over more pages, Tobias paused to study the chapter on the Pluto ley lines in Dallas. The myth of the Little Bear, or guardian of the Big Bear, struck karmic chords with the assassination. Though Khrushchev, the leader of the largest country with descendants of the Bear clan, and the US president desired world peace, the planet remained a center of conflict. Their death and exile implied an attack from the celestial realm. The US president had to hibernate or become still to learn the secret of freeing one's self before the planet could be free.

A notice appeared inside a crystal orb located in Bilbo's living room. Bilbo looked up and examined the reflections emanating from within the refracted layers of amethyst. He held the ball in his arms for a brief moment before deciding, "Gentlemen, you must hurry back to Iron Mountain. There's a red alert. Aliens are attempting to exploit the Schumann-wave guide."

Joe and Tobias repacked their bags and hurried out of the hut after donning a pair of Bilbo's goggles. Scurrying past the wasteland, they met Michelle waiting impatiently for them at the entrance to the tunnel. She lightly tapped Joe on the wrist, "Abraham wants you at the electronics panel. Tobias, you are needed at the base station. We have casualties."

Puzzled by the sudden turn of events, Tobias and Joe glanced at each other before running through the corridors. They hugged each other in the hallway by the conference room and went separate ways. Michelle accompanied Joe up the stairs to the panel. Abraham remained curiously absent from the device that he had once protected from Joe's interest. Michelle turned a key and lifted the top lid off the instrumentation. Joe ran his fingers of the device and studied the configuration.

"Serpentines infiltrated the Schumann wave guide long ago," he concluded. "Those using relying on alpha waves for communication and healing must exercise caution. Not all the information is trustworthy."

"I know, "Michelle said with a slight air of frustration. "We need to put the base and ourselves inside the eye of a hurricane. The chaos will leave a detectable magnetic imprint on our airships and we will be discovered."

"I think I can manage that," Joe said, hurriedly adjusting controls and bias. Pausing for a moment, he looked around the office for electronics supplies. He frantically pulled several drawers open. "I am looking for some wire of a particular alloy."

"I saw some cubits hanging in the broom closet over there," Michelle suggested. Running over to the closet, she grabbed several coils made of gold, silver, plutonium, titanium, and copper. "I recognized them when Abraham showed me around. Some of my colleagues use cubits for healing purposes."

Joe selected the plutonium cubit and twisted it into another design. With a screwdriver on his pocket knife, he lifted a section of the panel to expose the wiring and crystals underneath the control top. His hands moved over the array until he found the energy abnormality and placed the cubit around it "This should degauss the airships and ourselves. Apparently, our movements within the Mid-Earth created some permanent dipole moments, which were transferred to different stations connected to the Bilbo's hut." Stopping to reflect for a moment, he observe the peaceful mountain scenery outside the window. "Bilbo must have friends on other mountain tops."

Michelle smiled. "It keeps him going."

Abraham appeared from the stairwell. Having overhead some of their conversation, he added, "Not mountains, but Nazca lines. Bilbo connects to the Lizard design, which provides a transport system."

"Transport system?" Joe questioned.

"Serpentine forces penetrated the MidEarth during the Spirit Lake Massacre in 1857. Caves around the lake lead to the MidEarth. Traitors on both sides of the massacre betrayed my namesake, the one who went on to become President Lincoln. Bilbo escaped through the Lizard portal, which also connects to the Native American sites underneath Los Angeles."

"What happened?" Michelle asked.

Abraham explained how the Transylvania Land Company passed the Indian Removal Act in 1837 as Wilkinson agents laid tracks for the railroad in Illinois. The Seven Councils of Fires relocated to the Tetons and closed the opening in 1862. They chased the group of Armenian missionaries from Constantinople back to New York. Their physicians met the Rush organization in Philadelphia and established the Mayo Clinic, which seized Civil-War dead. Those bearing the Davenport coat of arms in Iowa intended to exercise control over spirits in the afterlife. They used occultists stationed at Pike Island near Fort Snelling, Minnesota to extend the Davenport hangman's noose to the spiritual realm. Since feudal times, the Davenport shield bore the hanged man's noose as a way of controlling the life and death of conquered European natives. In the New World, the Serpentine sought to regained their footing in the celestial realms and requested help from Albert Pikes's Knights of the Golden Dawn. The robber barons funding the operation adopted the Blue Cross of the Teutonic Knights, who drove immigrants out of their homeland and into the New World for further victimization. Cabals from Narnia and Armenia, remnants of those Persian princes running world empires, worked with the Hudson Bay Company to create news tribunes. The New York Tribune shared information with another tribune in Chicago and disseminated information for those operating British spy rings. Pulitzer and his other cohorts formed a club on Jekyll Island to educate the masses. Eventually, Robert Louis Stevenson penned a post-Civil War coverup called

Dr. Jekyll and Mr. Hyde, which portrayed the Jekylls as the good-natured side of the medical coinage.

Before his presidency, Lincoln established a homeopathic college, which championed traditional medicine against the upcoming military practice of selling human remains to colleges funded by robber barons. Pulitzer's Lincoln Calvary in New York spied for the Confederacy. His missionary friends in the newspaper business and press clubs directed the assassination. The media controlled an actor's success and they pulled the puppet strings on the Dionysus cult in the theaters.

"After the Roman Empire eliminated midwifery, most women died delivering their babies," Michelle commented after Abraham's discourse. "Military medicine is another form of warfare or genocide, perhaps more specifically gender-cide."

Abraham added, "Thirty years following the Civil War, the military massacred many Armenians and destroyed Persian medicine. Highly skilled refugees brought the knowledge to northern India."

Tobias emerged from the stairwell. Appearing weary from addressing the wounds of the airship crews, he dripped water from his recent shower onto the wood floor. His shirt clung to his skin in wet patches and he ran his fingers through his hair to dry it with heat from his palms. Stepping away from the small puddle beneath his hiking boots, he continued the thread of the conversation, "After the Persians conquered Greece, the Romans seized Persia and placed their generals in power. In 1894, the descendants of Roman soldiers exerted their influence again."

Michelle added, "My colleague studied with an Unani doctor in Pakistan. Unlike Western Medicine, continuity exists between the medicine prescribed for someone like Alexander the Great and today's tourist. They use aromatherapy to cool their homes instead of air conditioners, which are based on Tesla's World War II technology."

Tobias kissed Michelle's cheek and raised one eyebrow with a sigh. "Never underestimate the power of scent."

Michelle commented, "The ancient Hebrews used electromagnetism for healing long before the Romans replaced their medicine with Hippocrates."

"Their Serpentine sponsors didn't want the natives to use the Schumann-wave guide," Tobias quipped.

Discovered in the 1950's, the United States government confirmed the existence of a layer in the atmosphere that could conduct electromagnetic waves around the globe. An ancient civilization created the layer to support communication between levitated base stations. When Serpentines used radio waves to exterminate the Arctos, the civilizations levitated a handful of survivors to safety. One of the survivors emigrated to Druid settlements and started a new school of physicians. A graduate named Merilyn, the wizard often mistaken in Roman history as Merlin, brought the culture of his forebears forward through a pupil called Arcas. Arcas became the father of King Arthur, which meant bear in the English language. Roman history considers Arcas the same as King Arthur; but according to the Druids, the two men existed as separate, distinct individuals. The Romans consider the Pendragon as King Arthur's father, but the

Druids knew the Pendragon as the Turk from Constantinople. The Pendragon, a descendant of Gilgamesh, was a distant cousin of Arthur. One of Arthur's distant relations had chosen to marry Constantine's father and side with the Serpentines. Through an extensive gridding system exemplified at Stonehenge, the Bear clan thrived against the Serpentine electromagnetics ruining Greece, Persia, Rome, and Constantinople.

Representing the personification of the Serpentine invaders, the various Caesars failed to dominate the Druid settlements. It wasn't until the Greek goddesses of Fates intervened, that Constantinople ran over Northwestern Europe. Lachesis chose the time dimension of Cronus as a base of reference. The poison, which Lachesis weaved through the destinies of the conquered tribes, threatened the Light spirits from the MidEarth. The collection of Light Beings, the ones who had helped the inhabitants of Iron Mountain, evacuated to the confines of the MidEarth.

Chapter Nine

TOBIAS HEAVED A deep sigh and stared at the falcon soaring over them. The falcon belonged to Diana, the huntress. No one on Iron Mountain entertained the notion that she was goddess. Instead they pulled her from the wreckage of a burning spaceship and administered first aid. Tobias, as part of her parallel universe, stayed beside her until she closed her eyes during a final moment. Her falcon perched on the metal railing above her head. The bird flew away when she passed over.

Exhausted from his experience with the casualties at the base station, Tobias sat down on a log and wiped the tears from his eyes. Michelle knelt down beside him and stared into his eyes. She gently took his hand in hers.

"What's going on, Tobias?" she asked in soft voice.

"I feel like a failure," he admitted. "From what we've seen in the MidEarth, we were unsuccessful in protecting Iron Mountain."

Three groups saved the galaxy after the Serpentines destroyed the intergalactic pentagon. Iron Mountain provided air support and prevented further attacks on Gondwanaland. Scouts from Andromeda assisted the Pleiadian survivors and rallied against the M33 Arachnids intending to infest the entire planet. Gondwanaland operated spaceships for the soul transport system (STN) between earth and the Pleiades, also known as the godhead. The Seven Sisters of the

Pleiades constituted the divine feminine. They had been birthed on the same mountain as Mercury, Mount Cyllene. Targeted by the nephilim, the Seven Pleiades inhabited the center of the station. The celestials fought the intruders in heaven and on earth. When the Orion Council collapsed, the attackers focused on Gondwanaland. Iron Mountain rescued a Titan named Atlas and Zeus II's daughter Diana. Atlas founded Atlantis as a refugee base. Like Diana, Abraham, Tobias and Michelle lived in the same parallel universe through astral projection and kept their connection to the celestials. These celestials consisted of souls, which had endured repeated attacks from the nephilim. Joe, an earth-born soul, descended from Metratron, also called Enoch. Lacking the connection to the celestial, Joe wasn't as busy as the other souls, who had a network of friends elsewhere. Metatron's ascendance shaped the two parallel universes by separating the two realities. This protective measure gave some souls the option of two playing fields, in case one became uninhabitable. Noah did not come from Metatron/Enoch, though his progeny nourished a celestial connection, which the nymph Maia knitted with a divine illusion. The divine illusion protected Psyche, the personification of the mortal soul who took flight with Eros, the son of Mercury cultivating love for the devastated earth.

The nephilim competed with life on earth and forged a third reality, which proved illusory. Sorcerers by nature, the fallen ones failed to 'walk the talk" like Noah's descendants sporting a divine illusion for their benefit. When Eden fell, Eve's children possessed a self-destructive programming wrought by the Serpentines's input into the knowledge base. Noah and the survivors on the ark cleared the self-destructive programming and replaced the vacuum with a survival pattern. The diffracted light of the rainbow cleared the original programming. All of Eve's descendants required reprogramming, which differs from the mind-control features of the Serpentine agenda.

Tobias glanced at the falcon in the sky. Joe had already left the porch to track its flight down the mountain. Silently, Abraham, Michelle, and Tobias watched him go. They snacked and rested in the sunshine during his departure. An hour later, Joe returned with an expression of elation.

"The falcon showed me another way to get to the MidEarth. I watched it disappear into a crevice. When I peered into the Earth's cavity, I noticed smoke rising from Bilbo's hut in the distance."

Tobias jumped to his feet and heartily hugged Joe. "The soul transport system works!"

Joe stared at Michelle. "Huh?"

"The falcon carries the spirit of Diana, the goddess of childbirth," Michelle told him. "Her spirit in the MidEarth will help recovery efforts."

Abraham waved at Joe and led him to a ravine on the other side of the office. Tobias followed them, while Michelle went inside to inquire about plans for dinner. Showing Joe a plant nested in the bog of the ravine, he said, "The Pitcher Plant integrates instinctive nature with astral forces. This carnivorous plant knows how to survive the intense, dark competition of life in a bog."

"Noah must have relied on it before drifting out-of-sight," Joe commented. "How do you reprogram those stuck in the Fall of Eden?"

"Raindrops," Michelle answered as joined them at the edge of the trail. "And other forms of scattered, rhythmic music. Affirmations and various forms of Jungian sand play or homeopathy."

"Raindrops seem much easier," Joe observed. After pausing for a brief moment, he asked, "If I am the only one amongst us not in a dual reality, then where do I go while you visit celestials?"

"The celestials come to you," Abraham replied. "Like those at Iron Mountain, you sidestep the illusion."

Tobias searched the skies for anymore signs of the falcon. He told the others, "The bigger question is who betrayed Diana's squadron?"

Michelle shuddered as she thought about the answer to the question. Turning around, she set her sights on the trail leading back to the stone office. Tobias followed her and put his arm around her shoulders when he caught up with her.

"Aldebaran," Abraham murmured before starting his hike up the side of the mountain.

Standing firm in his position alongside the bog, Joe overheard Abraham's whisper and shook his head without lowering it. He turned and lingered on the edge of the ravine as he studied the rays of light transforming the shades of gray to bright greens and yellows. In the absence of conversation, several tree frogs began croaking from the underbrush. Joe knelt close to the ground to the action under a few ferns. Turning over a stone, he found several worms and centipedes hurrying for deeper dirt. He thoughtfully watched their wiggles and movements over the vegetated debris. Noticing the dramatic change in the angle of the sun beams across the bog, he straightened and walked up the steep slope.

Michelle and Tobias met Joe at the porch. The couple sat on the edge of the deck and stared at the juxtaposition of airborne versus earth-borne in the scenery. Tobias raised his hand and slapped his outstretched palm against Joe's flattened hand when he passed by. Opening the door of the stone structure, Joe went inside to review the control panel. Lifting the top of the apparatus, he searched the circuitry for any electromagnetic resonance that matched the frequencies from Aldebaran. After locating the source of the aberration, he rummaged through a side drawer filled with capacitors of various shapes and sizes. Unable to find what he needed, he began constructing his own variation out of foil and cardboard. He clipped it in the configuration and noted the readings above the dials. Walking onto the porch, Joe gazed in the direction of the base station. High in the sky overhead, he observed airships emerging from behind tuffs of clouds. Their motion in the atmosphere suddenly became erratic. The crafts wobbled in the air with sharp dips until they completely disappeared. Joe blinked and looked down at Tobias to see if he had noticed the same phenomenon.

Tobias nodded, "It is almost as if they evaporated."

"What?" Michelle asked, lifting her head from Tobias's shoulder. "What did I miss?"

"Joe got rid of our problem. I think they were from Aldebaran."

"That's nice, Joe," Michelle said nonchalantly as she put her head back down and relaxed.

Joe returned to the control panel and replaced the lid. Moments later, Abraham appeared from the stairwell. Without a word, he picked up a screwdriver and assisted Joe by tightening down a few bolts. Then Abraham opened the front door and called to the couple, "Let's get some dinner."

Tobias nudged Michelle from her light slumber and rose to his feet. After a few stretches, he followed the rest down the stairwell. A small buffet awaited them in the conference room, Tobias picked up a plate and helped himself to some fish and rice, before sitting down next to Abraham.

"Tell me what you know about the Hegelian dialectic? One of Bilbo's books referenced him concerning Aldebaran's attack on the Pleiades."

Abraham looked down at the food on his plate and reached for the pepper shaker. He answered simply, "All of the philosophers tried to account for Rousseau, who deviated from Hume. Unlike the others, Rousseau remained separate from the University system, which funded their professors with money from the same bankers supporting British companies during the American Revolution. Hegel greeted Napoleon with open arms. They enjoyed the same financiers."

"And Kant?"

"He created the Transcendentalist movement that swept American academia into the arms of the US Confederacies opposing the pre-existing Native American confederacies. It represented another banking scheme, which seized the nation's currency for the master-slave dialectic."

Tobias quietly finished eating as he thought about Abraham's words. Alone, he walked through the corridors leading to the Mid-Earth, while the others remained behind and savored their meal. Bilbo greeted him at the entrance with a pair of goggles. Tobias smiled as he put them on.

"I heard that you were coming," Bilbo told him.

"I figured someone at the base would tell you," Tobias said with a light grin. He joined Bilbo on the cleared trail to his hut. Inside the cozy home, he removed his glasses and accepted a cup of warm cider. Without further hesitation, he related the purpose of his visit. "Abraham told me about Hegel and the Phenomenologists. I met their descendants at a university in Dallas years ago. It is interesting how a phenomenon of the Protestant Reformation could merge into occultism of the Cathars."

"They're monarchists," Bilbo responded as he sipped his cider. "It isn't the same as an anarchist." Putting his cup down for a few minutes, he reached for a book on the nearby coffee table and thumbed through a few pages. "Sparta, in ancient Greece, served as the template for drafting conquered tribes into Roman armies."

Changing the subject as he ran across a picture of Godin Tepe in Caspia, known today as western Iran. "I understand that you unravelled Metatron's Cube during your college days. Look at this, the Godin Tepe connects to the Goblecki Tepe in Turkey. King Arthur's paternal grandfather came from Finland. The Lapland people called him Ryan Casper. Ryan Casper's mother, a Caspian, ran operations at

Godin Tepe. The civilization raised a breed of small horses, which served the same purpose as the mustang for the Apache. The Apaches cultivated a post-pyramid group of survivors and became a distinct race."

Tobias thought for a moment. He responded, after gulping his warm brew. "The major pyramid civilizations fabricated crystals from the information gleaned from Metraton's Cube. The intergalactic Pentagon stored their knowledge in the shape of a icosahedron and told Mercury to give the object to Metatron. The Goblecki Tepe artisans carved cuboidal bowls made of sapphire. The attribute they imbued in the blue crystal resonated with the attribute of prosperity."

"Not a bad idea," Bilbo remarked with a hint of impatience in his manner. He shifted uncomfortably in his chair. "So King Arthur's grandmother concerned herself with prosperity. You can see it in the eyes of the splendid horses running wild around the Caspian Sea. They are shape-shifters and cannot be taken. King Darius of Persia only found a hybrid when he raced his chariots through the country."

Tobias put down his cup and changed the subject. Getting to the point of the circumlocution, he questioned, "So the monarchists gave the US to Pakistan after the Lincoln assassination?"

"The Mehrgarh rule the country. Hades daughter, Macaria, established their civilization long before Darius arrived on the scene."

"She personifies the notion of a blessed death. Before the Civil War, Lincoln's friends in the poetry business referred to it as 'taken from the fire yet to come.'"

"Oh yes, Edgar Lee Masters epitomized Macaria in *Spoon River Anthology*. The only other reference is in the *Suda*, which came out in the falling Byzantine Empire before William the Conqueror began razing English shires. The result became known as the Dark Ages."

Tobias immediately rose to leave. He told Bilbo, "That's all I need to know. Lincoln and the other dead of the Civil War served as a blessing. It got us out of hell."

"The monarchists from the Rome club in Narni worship Dionysus. Their practice represents the will of the gods, rather than the interests of the Earth. After the invaders destroyed the divine feminine at Gondwanaland, Gaia no longer had a voice."

Chapter Ten

1824

Vandalia, Illinois

CORNELIA OVERSAW ABRAHAM'S postal routes, which corresponded to the networks stemming from Fort Edwards. Though only fifteen years of age, Abe's height made him look much older. Captured by the Eagles during the American Revolution, the outpost proved to be the victory which kept the United India company out of the Ohio territory. Their protege in the White House developed a doctrine extending the company's jurisdiction to the West coast. The Spanish missionaries resented the intrusion and sought alliances with burgeoning Napoleonic forces in Mexico. John Shay often met Abraham along the route forged by Franklin and his grandson Benjamin Bache. Relations of Deborah Reed took over Bache's work after he succumbed to yellow fever during Napoleon's sudden rise to power.

Cornelia continued meeting John secretly in the hallways and kitchen of the Vandalia hotel. Sara, Abraham's older sister, joined the ranks of the Sparrows and assisted Lyman Beecher with his schools. Unlike the Ducks, Eagles, and Peacocks, the Sparrows distanced themselves from the war zone and became custodians of knowledge. While the Transcendentalists discouraged American intellectual pursuits, the Sparrows sought to educate themselves.

Taking the note from the tray that John Shay carried down the hall, Cornelia ducked into her room and read it. Between deliveries, Abraham stayed with John Shay in a tiny cabin in the backwoods behind the post office. This note bore the seal indicating that John had obtained the information from someone along Abraham's route. Sitting down on the bed, Cornelia ran her fingers over the wax seal as if to validate by feel what her eyes saw. Her fingers stopped and she closed her eyes. The wax seal bore another message, distinct from the handwritten one. A small groove located at the edge of purple seal told her that the Musketeers had another message for her. She opened the note without breaking the seal and read the inscription.

Ask Linkhorn about Iron Mountain

Cornelia folded the note and held it against the light of a candle. Looking through the blemish on the seal through flickering flame, she noticed the varying hues of purple. Another inscription appeared in tiny, bold black letters.

RETRIEVED AMETHYST NECKLACE FROM LADY CASTLEREAGH

Placing the note face done on the nightstand, Cornelia stared at her reflection in the mirror. Lady Castlereagh possessed the amethyst necklace until her demise. The popular British socialite used the necklace's crystals for communication with benevolent extraterrestrial forces, garnering support for her husband's forays in the

Vienna Council of 500. After succumbing to the cup of Borgia, Lord Castlereagh died from poisoning. He succeeded in countering Napoleon and funding the armies against the Holy Roman Empire. His efforts squashed the United India's invasion of the United States during the War of 1812. Lady Castlereagh directed popular support from the Carlisle House, where the financiers of the United India companies engaged each other in social obligations.

The Carlisle House pressured Bonaparte's government in Naples, Italy to arrest the French Musketeers in Naples. Castlereagh's success in Vienna threatened the Vatican's control of the Marco Polo's Silk Roads in Naples and Sicily. Da Vinci's Eagles supported Marco Polo's established routes and sought freedom from the United India companies. The result had been the American Revolution, though the roots reached as far back as the intergalactic wars of ancient Egypt. The cup of Borgia served the occult group, which sponsored Captain John Smith for the Transylvania Land Company. The occult cup allied themselves with the followers of Mirithism and created the Byzantine Empire. The Carlisle House represented the Roman legions left behind by Constantine and they still looked toward Rome for assistance.

Cornelia left the note for John Shay, who she knew would be entering the room after her departure. She opened the door and exited the hotel through the kitchen. Mounting her horse, she gazed at the glistening-silver path in the moonlight. Cornelia road out of town to an isolated cabin tucked in the woods fifteen miles away. Her horse whinnied at the small trail leading from the road to the hillside.

Abraham appeared out of the shadows and took the saddle off the horse. He hid it with all leather accoutrements from the horse beneath several large boulders. Cornelia made her way to the cabin in the distance as she felt the trees and branches for identifiable marks. At the door stood the wispy figure of an elder lady.

"Hello there, Miz Linkhorn," Cornelia whispered softly.

Youthful in facial appearance, Miz Linkhorn stepped out of the shadows and beamed at Cornelia with celestial light from the stars overhead. "I hear that you've come to learn about Iron Mountain."

"The Musketeers gave Pierre's amethyst necklace to the daughter of Captain Drake's old friend in Wales."

"Ah, good choice," Miz Linkhorn remarked as she offered a rocking chair on the porch to Cornelia.

Miz Linkhorn sat down on one of the steps and studied the constellations. When Abraham joined them on the porch, she nodded at Cornelia to continue.

An Orange fairy flitted in air around Cornelia, who curiously eyed the flying creature with apprehension. Abraham held out his finger and the Orange fairy perched in their midst. His beautiful, shiny, translucent wings slowed as he steadied himself. Ignoring the fairy, Cornelia focused her attention on her mission and asked, "What's the story behind Iron Mountain?"

"Long before the Serpentine invasion in Eden broke the Pangea supercontinent into Laurasia and Gondwanaland, a landmass called Kenorland became the base for extraterrestrials held as hostages."

Abraham pulled a hard, green ultramafic stone from his pocket. The Orange fairy disappeared into the dark woods and Abraham rose. Glancing in the direction of the vanishing fairy, he walked over to Cornelia and offered her the stone. Cornelia studied his face before opening her left hand, so that he could place it in her palm.

"It is serpentine," he said. "My mother told me about it. The books claim that it provides protection from the darkest kind of magic."

"Initially, the Linkhorns arrived on the planet as hostages," Miz Linkhorn interjected. "Nephilim brought them to this desolate planet, which served as holding tank for various intergalactic prisoners. Light Beings from other galaxies tunneled their way to the earth's core. They used light sabers and lazed past the hard bedrock to the molten core. Moving the openings in the bedrock underneath the nephilim's colonies, the Light Beings destroyed their bases with magma while the hostages dispersed and roamed the terrain. The Light Beings could morphed anywhere they wanted, whereas the Nephilim remained bound to their hideous structure."

A clap of thunder stopped Miz Linkhorn's narration. She left the exposed stairs and sought a chair under the eaves of the porch. Dry, white lightning streaked across the horizon in two compass directions. Taking his rock back from Cornelia, Abraham sought refuge under the roof of the porch. He found a rocking chair tucked in the back and at down far from the lightning. Cornelia remained calm in her seat at the edge of the porch and resumed rocking gently.

Miz Linkhorn surveyed the skies and continued, the Light Beings merged with the atmosphere around the planet, creating the

Thunder People. With the help of the freed hostages, they found forms on land and sea. New life forms, interjected with the love of the nomads and light of the Thunder People, took shape. When Serpentine forces invaded the Sun, the Sons of Heaven fled to a dead planet. The resulting flares from the Sun's atmosphere distorted the earth's electromagnetic sphere and created changes. Light Beings chose to make these changes positive and established mountain ranges on the North American continent. High on the mountains, the Linkhorns communicated with the Thunder People and maintained close contact as tensions in Atlantis mounted."

Cornelia sat back in her chair and drifted into the soft rhythm propelled by her own motions. The African plate collided with a European land mass and created the Swiss Alps. By this time the intergalactic pentagon had already been encapsulated in Metratron's Cube. Rather than return to the crystalized versions of the pyramid civilizations in Egypt and South America, the collective set up a station in a cavity of the Matterhorn.

The grandparent mountain of the Matterhorn, Mon Bosa, served as the base station for the Eagles that Da Vinci reorganized to guard the Spice Route. Sailors looked to the celestial heavens to navigate their ships. The Eagles used the mountain to communicate with the descendants of the Anasazi on the North American continent. The interplay of weather and the mountain's atmosphere reflected patterns created by the Zuni's pueblo dwellings. Their transmuted smoke signals hung in the sky, like the versions manifested by the Arctos survivors in the Himalayas.

The mandala for the world rose at Mount Kailash in Tibet, the result of more recent changes than Iron Mountain, though older than the Matterhorn. Serving as the source of many sacred rivers, the heights of the mountain fed the valleys below. For this reason, the name of the mountain translated into *crystal* for some civilizations as it broadcasted peace on earth and good will. Famine and lack fueled skirmishes; greed promoted wars, ironically threatening the existence of the embattled through gradual destruction of the mountain.

While the descendants of Eden struggled with their self-inflicted wounds with self-created dramas such as *Cain versus Able* and *Sodom and Gomorrah*, those living with the mountain and not *on it* sidestepped the resulting washouts plaguing humanity. When the sons of Abraham, the Hebrew prophet, decided to mimic the earth-bound peaks with a high rise in Babel, the population at Iron Mountain told them that it was a bad idea. With the ongoing tumult in intergalactic realms, such an artificial structure would broadcast the wrong message. Rather than say *I told you so* after an alien spaceship scattered the sons of Abraham into power-driven Brahmins, Iron Mountain put up a shield and isolated itself from the avarice. Da Vinci looked toward Iron Mountain for inspiration in promoting sustainable trades on the Silk Road and Spice Route, which the alien sponsors seized from Marco Polo and gave to enemies of the Brahmins, such as the nazim. The captain of the ship which destroyed the Tower of Babel worked with a dark wizard from Atlantis, known as Shazam. Together, they infused a segment of humanity with a gold fever, and those with lowered immunity to the infection became the nazim.

Abraham twirled a small stick between his fingers and passed the object deftly from hand to hand. As the stem sparkled in the moving light of the moon and stars, he waited for the return of the Orange fairy, who might be lured by his playful demonstration. When the fairy did not accept his bait, Abraham lowered the stick after a few seconds. He sighed in resignation and rejoined the adult conversation. His grandmother looked down at him. With a gentle, self-contained smile, she nodded her satisfaction and resumed.

"The abbess stationed at Sassafras Mountain told me about the alien invasion on the Texas Gulf coast almost fifteen years ago, about the time young Abraham was born in Alabama."

Sassafras Mountain, the highest peak in South Carolina, provided refuge for those wishing to escape the trafficking of the Transylvania Land Company and their methods, where the shedding of blood fueled their enterprises. Avalon relocated to the summit long before Captain John Smith surveyed the region for the company. When the minions of the vampirish Roman legions handed the territory to John Spencer to manage, he simply overlooked the abbey and its coeds.

Abraham stared at his grandmother when she mentioned his delivery. The Orange fairy returned from the forest and sat down on his should after a few flutters. Abraham remained awestruck by his grandmother's recollections of events, tying his personal life with pertinent intergalactic details. Briefly he glanced at the Orange fairy as if looking for a reality check. Focused on the discussion, the Orange fairy merely stood attentively at his side and grinned.

His grandmother announced to the group assembled, "We have our work cut out for us. Iron Mountain is preparing for the upcoming Mexican-American War. Extraterrestrial ships have ramped up operations and training at Iron Mountain."

Cornelia studied the starry-lit sky and searched for signs of life. Seeing a few identified flying objects slip through the constellations, she remarked, "The Grays keep insisting on keeping us under city light, where we can't see what is going on. These days it takes a trained eye to get the message."

Abraham rose after hearing her comment and decided, "I need to get back to town. They'll need some help at the store before it gets too late." Turning toward Cornelia, he mentioned, "I'll come at dawn to see you off on your journey."

After hugging and kissing them both farewell, he disappeared down the path. As Abraham skipped through the lush vegetation, the Orange fairy muted his colors and blended with the shadows crossing the ride on Abraham's lithe frame. Cornelia stayed the night with Miz Linkhorn and drew up plans for the krewe at Annapolis, which needed to seize a few harbors on the West coast. The krewe referred to the sailors who enjoyed partying with the Cajuns on the Gulf Coast. They worked with the native peoples and represented the US government before the United India company created another version of affairs.

"We'll ask the Sea Dragons frolicking in the waters near the Redwoods to escort the ships to the harbor at San Diego," Miz Linkhorn decided. "Extraterrestrial ships from Iron Mountain can cloak the entry. The Kumeyaay tribes already have several members in the krewe."

The next day Cornelia left for Fort Edwards, where she intended to meet with officers from Annapolis and Springfield, Massachusetts. Abraham met her at the cabin and helped her find her way back to the road. The sun had not risen yet, though streaks of burgeoning light casted bluish hues over the brush. He had already retrieved her saddle from its hiding place between the rocks. Her horse silently waited for her in the shadows of the towering rocks. Wisps of vapor emanated from animal's snout and hung in the air. Cornelia rubbed the horse's face in delight, softly kissing the living and breathing animal, which would be her traveling companion for the next few desperate days. She tightened the ropes on the horse and checked her gear. Satisfied, she mounted and waved at Abraham as she briskly turned the horse in the direction of the trail. She left him as if she expected to see him again soon.

Abraham watched her go, bowing his head and acknowledging that she had failed to tell him goodbye. Scuffing away the footprints, he acted as if he knew that she only had room in her heart for hellos. He turned in another direction and made his way back to the store, while the dark blues turned into crisp yellows and crimson.

Stopping at various familiar outposts and entering through the kitchens, Cornelia dodged the attention of bounty hunters and traders. It only took her a few seconds to assume the appearance of any ol' hired hand or servant, the type of people that didn't matter to the establishment causing the problems in the conflicted young nation. She entered the confines of Fort Edwards with a wagon train carrying supplies. The orderly recognized her and quietly ushered her to the main office. The captain of the fort brought her a cup of hot tea as Cornelia warmed herself near the potbelly stove. He accepted the documents from her hands and sat down at his desk to review.

"Miz Linkhorn must be really happy to get her grandchildren back," he commented as he folded a note.

"Yes, their parents put their hopes and dreams for the new country with their given names, Abraham and Sara," Cornelia remarked as she undid her scarves and sat down on a stool. "They wear them well and are eager to do their part."

The sound of gunfire abruptly interrupted their conversation. The captain rose from his desk and grabbed several pistols. Handing one to Cornelia, he directed her to a secret tunnel that led outside the fort. Cornelia buried the gun in her loose scarves and made her way behind him in the dimly lit passageway. At the end of the path, he opened a heavy metal door, allowing cracks of sunshine to mark their exit.

"You go that way and I go this way. Susan Anthony teaches at the local school and she was told to expect you. I must rejoin the ranks before the official commanding officer arrives."

Chapter Eleven

CORNELIA DEPARTED FROM the doorway without looking back. Instead of showing up at the schoolhouse, she went to her younger brother's house. Charlie's head rose slightly above the curtains as she stepped onto the porch. He briefly peered through an opening between the hems of the checkered cloth and rushed to swing the door open, leaving her no time to make a knock. She laughed in delight when he swept her in his arms with a mighty hug that twirled her over the threshold. Shutting and locking the entrance behind them, he took her by the hand and led her to a stronghold beneath the hallway floor.

Cornelia descended the stairs and entered a cellar-like room full of people. Still holding her hand, her brother made polite introduction, "You'll find Susan Anthony here too. They let out school when the fighting started."

A small girl stepped forward and shook Cornelia's hand. "I'm Susan Anthony. Let's talk."

Cornelia eyed her brother, before nodding her reply. "I made it just underneath the wire." Then she composed herself and smiled slightly at the young woman, who appeared to be no older than ten years old. "The Sparrows sent me."

Bowing her head, the young woman pulled away from the group. "I understand."

Charlie broke the mood. He wryly interjected, "All women, the young and the old, hide their ages these days. Susan expressed a desire to be educated, so we let her be the teacher for the outpost. We have a lot to learn."

Susan brightly lifted her head and eagerly nodded her agreement. Cornelia found a seat on a bench and rummaged through the knapsack, which she had hid under her cloak. Her pistol remained concealed in her scarves. Finding what she needed in the bag, she produced a small book and handed it to Susan. "It came from Nancy Hank's collection. You'll find no other like it in the public libraries."

Susan accepted the book and thoughtfully examined the cover. She murmured, *"Columns: Women's History in the Face of Roman Legions."* After caressing the text and running her fingers over the volume, the young woman clutched the book against her breast as she closed her eyes. Susan breathed as if she could inhale the contents, then she found a chair near a lighted candle and started reading.

Cornelia and the others let her be. Someone in the sunken enclosure commented, "Susan already has a strong group of constituents. Her sensitive, youthful approach brings her many students."

Charlie drew his sister aside. He showed her a map on the wall. Rising his right index finger, he instructed, "The next base is east of Erie, Pennsylvania. The Reeds have a militia there. We need reinforcements in town. Our ruse at Fort Edwards is coming to a close. We need to let the United India company believe they run the place, otherwise we attract unwanted attention. Patrick of Ireland termed the maneuver, Transparency."

Without a word, Cornelia accepted Charlie's game plan. She moved toward the stairs as she gathered her belongings. Charlie silently whisked her out of the stronghold and through the trapdoor. Embracing her before opening the front door for her, he whispered in her ear, "A soldier from the fort tied your horse outside the gate."

Cornelia walked away from the wood-frame house and found her horse as Charlie promised. Quickly she checked the ropes and stored her gear. The fort had refreshed her supplies and given her a map to the Erie base. Glancing up and down the vacant streets to assure herself that no one watched her movements, she hurried out of town and directed her horse in the opposite direction of the distant battle.

Some Seneca Indians met her on the old trade route called the Venago Path. When the Columbus company claimed the trail as their own, Da Vinci's Eagles arrived to protect the passageway. They joined the French fur traders and spied on the Hudson Bay company. After establishing several outposts in a chain along the route, they regained the Fort Pisque Isle and defeated those occultists bottling the Florida water, which Ponce de Leon dubbed the Fountain of Youth. The Senecas took Cornelia to a barge at the water's edge. They poled the craft across the river to the encampment on Pisque Isle.

Cornelia shuddered as the wind nipped across the icy waters. When they reached the opposite shore, several frontiersmen rode toward Cornelia and escorted her. Inside the fort, Cornelia dismounted and tied her horse in the stable. She went through a secret passageway that led to a chamber under the kitchen. A shower of warm water streamed from a crevasse in the ceiling. Seneca Indians handed her a blanket as she undressed and headed for the mineral spray. An inscription on the wall caused her to gasp. Frantically, she ran her fingers over the letters as torrents dropped past her head and shoulders to the shale floor. Prying a rock free from a tiny ledge, she unearthed a labradorite crystal. With the rock clutched tightly in her right palm, she stepped away from the waterfall and wrapped the blanket around her.

Placing the crystal down on a nearby bench, Cornelia finished dressing. Then she grabbed the stone and left the room for a spiral staircase behind a dumbwaiter.

"Here," she announced to the uniformed waiter standing at the kitchen counter. The labradorite crystal gleamed from her open palm. "It is a stone of transformation. It's eerie. I saw the script on the wall. They wrote in Hungarian, a dialect of the Ur in Transylvania. If you want to learn what is going on, learn Hungarian."

The waiter took the stone from her and bowed his head. "They didn't name Erie, Pennsylvania for the natives." Rubbing the stone between his fingers, he slowly lifted his head. He resolutely eyed Cornelia. "The writing confirms our suspicions regarding Penn's activities with Ur. We are battling illusionists, sorcerers of the nephilim."

Cornelia turned around and leaned against the counter. "These sorcerers don't like water, do they?"

"They are washouts," the waiter recollected as he looked down at the labradorite. "How did you know to look for the labradorite?"

"It is an old musketeer trick," she replied. "It communicates with the civilization on Iron Mountain. One of the Huron Indians must have placed it on the ledge when they recaptured the fort. Only a few of the Erie Indians survived the illusionists' mind-poison. The Senecas took them in."

"What next?" the waiter asked.

"I need to go back to Dixie and check with the descendants of the Anasazi," she answered. "When does the next barge leave for the Mississippi River?"

He checked with the supply master sitting in the next room. Cornelia walked over to the kitchen stove and assisted the cook, who asked her to stir the pots while she added more kindling to the wood-burning stove. After a brief discussion in the supply office, the waiter returned and offered Cornelia some fresh bread with a bowl of beef stew. Joining her for lunch at a small table, he disclosed, "The supply master told me about the complications."

To avoid being overheard, the waiter scribbled a note for Cornelia. She looked over his shoulder and read:

Richard Bache, Jr. can get you around Dallastown, Pennsylvania.

Cornelia nodded her understanding and the waiter tore the paper into tiny pieces before tossing in the fire of the wood-burning stove. The pendulum clock in the room chimed on the hour. She looked out the window and noticed a man ride into the fort. He tied his horse to post outside of the captain's office and went inside to deliver his parcel. Cornelia waved at the supply master in the next room as the waiter helped her gather her things. Mounting her horse, Cornelia saw the waiter secure an extra bag of supplies near the reins. She lightly touched his hand in gratitude and rode out of the compound with the postal service.

When they had reached the trail in the dense woods, the man spoke, "How is young Abe getting along these days?"

"He's working with the Basques on the postal route to New Foundland. They settled with the natives long before the Columbus company enslaved the southern tribes. The Basques sailed with Columbus and got the word out to the rest."

Reaching to touch a gold leaf hanging on a tree limb, he responded, "After they murdered Bennie, his newspaper route seeded another underground delivery trail. They forced me to marry Dallas's sister, otherwise we all would be shanghied to China for purposes of world trade."

"How's the Missus?" Cornelia asked.

"Oh, do you mean the Mises?" Richard joked with chagrin. Mises referred to the economic philosophy cultivated by the relations of Ur in Austria. "Like all arranged wedlocks, we share a common enemy," he commented. "Wars create strange bedfellows, usually untrustworthy in matters concerning blood."

Cornelia laughed with his jest. "I am very lucky to have my man in Annapolis."

Richard winked at her. "That you are, ma'am."

Together, they turned down a deserted road. Cornelia mentioned, "My father told me about Dallas when I lived in Jamaica. They lived a mile outside of town."

An uncomfortable silence ensued. Taking a deep breath, Richard reflected for a moment and added, "Now that Madison's war has ended, Dallas's son is setting himself up along native trade routes in the Texas territory. I am working with Sam Houston to bring in the territory under the Eagle's safeguard, otherwise our freedom here is threatened."

"And the Second National Bank," she remarked, eyeing Richard.

He gulped, "After William Jones captured Fort Pisque Isle, Madison and the roman triumvirate in the senate conceded. Now that Jones is running the bank, departed members of the senate such as Dallas intend to run the currency out from right underneath him."

"Yes, our war is with company traders in the south and west."

Their conversations continued intermittently throughout their journey and they parted ways after reaching Iron Mountain, Arkansas.

Chapter Twelve

CORNELIA MET WITH the refugees surrounding Iron Mountain. Tiny shacks hidden between the trees in the forest housed hordes of people. They told her about the tortures at Fort Smith, the military outpost located on the Arkansas River. The soldiers broke up families, sending the men into saloons and the women into brothels. Those running the Dallas settlement owned the brothels as well as the saloons. The locals named Fort Smith, *Hell on the Border*.

Ouachita natives from northern Louisiana listened to the group and offered assistance. They took Cornelia to the base station on Iron Mountain, where she consulted with the others freed along with Abraham Linkhorn. She showed them the labradorite crystal from the fort near Erie, Pennsylvania.

A military officer doubling as an agent for the Spanish empire named Fort Smith in honor of his relation. The aide had helped General Wilkinson discard Jefferson's vice-president when he failed to create a war with Mexico. Instead, they called themselves patriots and supported the roman triumvirate in the senate.

"We have the same problem brewing around Spoon River, Illinois," Cornelia observed. "The army's chief of engineers, the one who covered up the betrayal at West Point along with Washington, is setting up internment camps."

"Our agent at West Point, Edgar Allen Poe, won't be able to hold out much longer," one of the women at the base station speculated. "He told Lafayette about the situation."

"Lafayette also met with President Monroe during his trip to the United States," a man in the group commented. "Monroe is just another University monarchist."

Cornelia left the discussion and strode over to the airships docked at the base station. Inspecting the troops by the ships, she ordered them to attack Fort Smith. They hurried to fulfill their mission and returned several hours later.

"Wilkinson's Grays raced for Fort Gibson. There aren't many survivors," an officer reported to Cornelia as she packed for Dixie.

Satisfied with the results of the operation, she instructed one agent to alert the postal service and add Fort Smith to the system. Then she departed with the Ouachita natives for the Oklahoma territory. Several weeks later, she arrived at an Anasazi encampment.

Buried deep in the canyons of red rock, the isolated cliff dwellers remained isolated from the local natives. Several women and a man greeted her when she arrived. The Ouachita natives stayed behind several hundred yards as Cornelia conferred with the Anasazi. After a few hours, she rejoined her Ouachita escorts and they headed for an Apache encampment forty miles away.

The Apaches transformed the dying pyramid civilizations into a new nation, seeded off the Gulf coast. After aliens sacrificed the natives in an occult ritual, their spaceships blasted the scene of the crime into tiny grains of sand. Dust-like remnants of stone temples washed on the present-day Mustang Island. Only a handful of

South American natives made their way to a port in Peru, where a benevolent spaceship took them to Mustang Island. The refugees created a new nation, calling themselves Apaches. The formed strong ties with the wild horses, which became known as mustangs. They traded with the Cocomamas in South America for chocolate.

When Columbus arrived with his crew, the Basques remained behind as slaves. Masters at seafare, their relations in the Pyrenees worked with the Eagles at Annapolis during the American Revolution. They supported Lafayette during the French Revolution. One of Cornelia's contacts in Puerto Rico managed to free a family of Basque slaves. Her agent Rodrigquez united the youngest son with his Ardanza relations in France. The others fled to the Maine outpost, where Abraham Linkhorn served as a mail carrier. Years later, the son returned to Caracas and ousted the Spanish royals with assistance from Fort Edwards and the Cocomamas. His aide, the nephew of an Irish general, gave him a copy of the Eagle's documents concerning the American Revolution. Developed by the Blue Herons, the original Declaration of Interdependence and constitution had eventually reached Lafayette through Benjamin Franklin's postal routes. Lafayette had given the documents to Rousseau's nephew, who gave the documents to General O'Leary in Sweden. General O'Leary gave another copy of the Blue Heron's documents to his nephew to give to the Basque son, Simon Bolivar.

One of the Apache women handed Cornelia a Dixie note. Accepting the bill, Cornelia remarked, "The Dallas occult lodge in Pennsylvania fund their own people in the Second National Bank. They want to use the bills created by John Wilkes's Hellfire Gang."

During his stay in England, Benjamin Franklin became a member of the Hellfire Gang, while under the influence of his first wife, an occultist with the Roman Empire in Armenia. After the War of 1812, Philadelphia became divided between Dallas's occult lodge and the Amalgamators led by James Buchanan. During the War of 1812, George M. Dallas worked for his father, the Secretary of the US Treasury. His brother used the war as an excuse to seize Annapolis's bases near Galveston. They overran the naval station and captured Pierre Lafitte, the man who escaped to Bowling Green, Kentucky to consult with Bilbo concerning the MidEarth. A. J. Dallas declared himself commodore of the US Navy there and began fueling the Puerto Rican Independence movement. Like Wilkinson and Madison, the freedom fighters rebelled against the royals in favor of the corporate oligarchs from Narnia. Betrayed by Jose Maria Rojas, Bolivar's Venezuela natives became tied to the Puerto Rican Independence Movement.

The namesake of Galveston, Galvez had served as a governor of the Louisiana territory and smuggled supplies to the Eagles during the American Revolution. A predecessor, Unzaga, became Captain General of Venezuela and assisted Bolivar's family. Unzaga's predecessor, O'Reilly worked with Pierre. Two years earlier, a relation of Lafayette, General Henri La Fayette Holstein failed to seize Puerto Rico from the man who had imprisoned him in Cadiz, Spain. Recently, the two had been reunited during Lafayette's trip to the United States. William Jones, became Secretary of the Navy after the War of 1812 and replaced Dallas as Secretary of the Treasury. Using Pierre's and Lafayette's insights gleaned by unravelling Metatron's Cube, Jones presided over the Second National Bank of the United States. They designed the bank to appeal to the fairy kingdom for help, as the fairies took over the soul transport network. By 1828, Henri La Fayette felt compelled to distance himself from Bolivar and the struggle in Venezuela. Two years later, Bolivar died from military medicine while in exile. His aide, O'Leary assumed operations in Colombia. In 1836, the Second National Bank closed its doors.

Seeking the shade of a grove of oaks, Cornelia sat down on a straw mat with the Apache emissaries. She examined the Dixie more closely and noticed that the currency had been minted in Stephen F. Austin's settlement. Working as an empresario, Austin secured American holdings north of the Alamo. Another one of Patrick Henry proteges, Austin managed to obtain a degree from Transylvania University in Kentucky. The degree allowed him to work as a double agent after the dictator, Santa Ana, abolished the constitution in favor of Dallas's forces along the Gulf. Like the Sants left behind by Constantine in Europe, Santa Ana represented the in-terests of the Roman legions. These legions in Armenia favored the US dollar laced with the Egyptian occultism practiced by Franklin's first wife.

A hawk soared overhead. Deciding to keep their discussion brief, Cornelia told them, "We must not linger in this place of war. Dallas's brother-in-law can help Sam Houston and Austin manage affairs in Texas. Henri La Fayette holds the reins in Pennsylvania."

Nobody responded to her words. Instead, they cocked their heads to listen to another sound. Within seconds a rider on a mustang appeared over the southern horizon. A cloud of dust followed the female shaman galloping swiftly toward them. A light, thin turquoise veil flew in the wind like a flag, shielding her long, dark hair from the dirt kicked up from her stallion.

"It's Lady Casper," the Apache man decided.

"I invited her," Cornelia mentioned.

Lady Casper quickly dismounted and hurried to the group, who rose to greet her.

"You must leave this place," she told them as she shook the dust from her clothes. "Separate and go hide in the next canyon. I'll get your funding from the Dragon flyers in Russia. They call themselves Cossacks."

Descended from the survivors of the Arctos, the Cossacks worked with the other inhabitants around the Caspian Sea. They ran operations at the Godin Tepe, where Lady Casper managed intergalactic communications. When the Castle Marlboro fell into alien hands, Lady Casper ascended with her flying dragon called Ea. Ea, the mother of Paisley and Gilderoy, now played a prominent role in another galaxy. Unlike the spiritual warriors of her grandson's kingdom in northern Europe, she had already fulfilled her contract to fight to the death in a previous lifetime. As the Apaches practiced intra-dimensional travel with their peyote rituals, Lady Casper peeled back the layers of time to assume new lifetimes without ever physically dying. She wandered into the mists and entered various scenes like an actress on the world stage. Her connections with the Cossacks earned her a place in the Russian royal court.

Her position on the world stage came with responsibility. Initially, females had dominated the planet. This came as a result of the

Pleiadian contract. The two gay kings in the Pleiades became the parents of seven females through a series of different birth mothers. During the intergalactic crisis, women bore the responsibility for the soul transport system between Gondwanaland and the Pleiadian godhead. After Gondwanaland became infiltrated by Hades's allies, some of the high priestesses sold out and became Gollums. Like the fallen hauflin in the Lord of the Rings trilogy, the aspirations of the populace degraded into obsessions. Male dominance over the planet emerged as the surviving female spirits shapeshifted. The women could turn into the white Caspian horses at will. Their caretakers at Godin Tepe guarded the female spirits under the watchful eye of Lady Casper, who waited patiently for the time when women could share power with men. Men needed to evolve to share responsibility in the soul transport system. None of these circumstances reflected intentional design, rather some called it an accident of nature, whereas the hardy individual gratefully considered the evolutionary tasks as another opportunity.

Cornelia and the others raced to the canyon as directed. Lady Casper rode ahead and met them near a spring-fed wading pool. In the glistening waters, they refreshed themselves and enjoyed the change from the desert heat. Some Ouachita scouts reported that a company of soldiers in gray uniforms had arrived at the oak grove shortly after their departure. Cornelia took a deep breath and watched several eagles soar over the surrounding cliffs. They resumed the discussion with Lady Casper offering further insights.

"The pyramid civilization of the Goblecki Tepe made cubes of sapphire from Metratron's Cube," she offered. "Toussaint Louverture, the black Spartacus of Haiti, showed O'Reilly and Pierre the sapphire necklace when they met in Cadiz."

Remembering the purpose of her mission, Cornelia sighed deeply and rummaged inside her nearby pack. She handed the Apaches several notes. "Here are Pierre's corrections for the sapphire cubes."

Though Toussanint succeeded in freeing Haiti from the Roman Empire, the feat cost him his life. The sapphire necklace went to his successor Petion, who handed it over to his lover Marie Madeleine Lachenais. As the president of two Haitian presidents, she initiated sweeping in the government of Haiti and protected the country from the Roman Empire. In 1815, she gave the necklace to Simon Bolivar when Petion offered him sanctuary. Bolivar gave the sapphire necklace to O'Leary before his death. O'Leary used the sapphire necklace to protect Colombia trade with the Apaches.

Two of the Apache women studied Pierre's notes. He wrote about his investigation with the emerald crystal from the Giza pyramid civilization. The green segment of Metatron's Cube indicated that Cronus, the progenitor of Hades and Zeus, programmed the planet for self-destruction. Pierre described the twofold solution for this embedded problem in the design of the pyramids.

Part of the answer concerned Germanicus, who came into possession of the emerald during his expeditions. The adopted son of the Roman Emperor, Germanicus sided with the Dragon flyers of northern Europe. Like Alfred the Great, he learned from the god Thor's mistakes. Thor went the way of many of the Greek and Roman deities and failed to incarnate on the planet due to ego issues. Kindness mattered most in the world. Germanicus and Alfred, called Alfie by his close friends, cultivated this attribute in their lives. Kindness made Germanicus invincible in his skirmishes with the Roman Empire.

Another part of the answer came from Germanicus directly. As a kindness, he left an inscription on the crown studded with Metatron's emerald crystal. He advised those reestablishing the intergalactic pentagon to *Cut the Fates*. The Fates consisted of three Greek goddesses: Clotho, Lachesis, and Atropos. Clotho provided the thread for life; Lachesis measured it; and Atropos cut it. Granddaughters of Cronos, the Fates ruined any individual's plans for ascendance or salvation.

Though Germanicus proved unable to change his own destiny, Pierre proposed several strategies for dealing with the Fates. For Clotho, he suggested finding a different thread, which took determination. He predicted that Lachesis would fade if one assumed a shamanistic approach. Transcendence, the ability to go beyond the limitations of the ancestors or culture, pertain to the shaman's world. Pierre proposed that Atropos, a fear-based entity, could be avoided by calming oneself and realizing that another's fate did not mirror one's own destiny.

Since the American Revolution, humanity had been blessed with the gift of choice. The minor decisions made during a life could result in a different thread measured by Zeus's daughters. By refusing to look at the passage of time as a river which ran the course of least resistance, a life could be altered through a decision-making process based on value.

Cornelia rose from her position on the grassy beach and wandered over to a willow. While the others discussed Pierre's findings, she rubbed the leafed twigs between her hands. Out of the corner of her eye, she saw the Apaches and Ouachitas nod in affirmation.

"Medicine," they softly murmured to Lady Casper.

She smiled back at them and communicated, "Medicine is the power of the human spirit."

In the morning, Lady Casper walked away from the camp and disappeared with the mustang. The vapor emanating from the dewy vegetation and springs concealed her departure through a portal leading to the Tsar's court. Having relinquished the country's claim to North America earlier in the year, the royal court bought itself more time to prepare for a confrontation with the Roman Empire.

Chapter Thirteen

ACCOMPANIED BY THE Ouachita natives, Cornelia journeyed a Native American settlement forming on the edge of Fort Smith. She joined them for an evening campfire and they told her about the Pike expedition in Colorado. Under orders of General Wilkinson, Zebulon Pike staked out the Rockies. Then he advised the natives to leave the area. Shortly after his departure, real estate agents with the Transylvania Land Company sent scouts to survey the region.

She left the next morning for Vandalia, Illinois where she passed information to various agents stationed at the hotel. They told her that the Dallas lodge started stocking the House of Representatives with 'WOLVES.' Cornelia reported that occultists from Transylvania had conjured Archons when they occupied Fort Pisque Isle near Erie, Pennsylvania. The WOLVES represented a German occult group. Though not at the level of a werewolf like their founder, Lycaon, these rabid individuals sought to carry out Lilith's mandate to annihilate the Fairy spirit.

"We don't need any education, especially when the most profitable commodity in China is opium" Cornelia retorted, throwing the report into the fire. She rose from the edge of her bed and stared at the flames leaping from the hearth. "The man who lost his tea and opium during the Boston Tea Party is reestablishing a base in Izmir, Turkey. The ancient Greeks called the place, the home of Homer."

"Yes, but the bard was blind," the waiter rejoined. Helping himself to a cup of water from the tray that he carried into the room along with the note, he glanced outside the window for signs of an eavesdropper. "Do you think that Zeus got to the poet?"

Cornelia never answered the question. Instead, she added, "Zebulon's relation just graduated from Harvard without attending classes. As I said, education is no longer valued."

"Though Franklin managed to sidestep the Hellfire Gang, other men in Philadelphia did not. One of the signers to the counterfeit Declaration of Independence started Brown University along with the post-revolution president of Yale."

A knock on the door interrupted the discussion. Both Cornelia and the waiter exchanged glances. They had not been expecting newcomers and had not been alerted by stationed guards.

"It's Lady Casper," a soft voice on the other side told them.

The agent opened the door and a waitress wearing a light turquoise-colored apron walked in. The shaded of blue and texture matched the veil that she had worn in Dixie. Lady Casper handed Cornelia some sealed documents.

Reviewing the notes as she continued to warm herself by the hearth, Cornelia summarized the report for agent waiting at the door. "The Pentarchy, which the Serpentines created in place of the intergalactic pentagon, intends to produce another Ivan the Terrible in the fifty years. They call the operation Rasputin."

"They apparently weren't pleased with Russia's withdrawal from North America," the agent speculated before eyeing Lady Casper for confirmation.

She nodded quietly. "They live off of wars. I am of no use in the Russian royal court."

Cornelia observed the sun shining outside the window. "It may take a hundred years, but we may be able to establish a Pentagon on this continent. We'll use the designs from Metatron's Cube and wait for our moment." She looked down and studied the ground beneath her feet. After pausing to reflect for a moment, Cornelia decided, "I must go to Annapolis and start them on these long-term plans."

Spending seven years in Annapolis, Cornelia devised strategies for the Pentagon. She continued meeting with Abraham Linkhorn on a regular basis. As many of the postmaster positions became filled by agents promoting the opium trade, Abe, as his friends called him, came to Annapolis in the winter of 1828. His sister, Sara, had married two years prior and died delivering a still-born baby. Living in Vandalia, there were no physicians available who would not blow her cover and alert the Thomas Lincoln network. Her spouse worked undercover at the hotel. He often fed Cornelia information on rendezvous. Grief stricken by the loss of the woman he loved, he urged Abe to return to the United States and formalize his education.

Abe chose the study of law, which he studied between shifts at the Annapolis docks, he studied law. His varied interests won him a broad circle of friends and instructors. The parents of Simon Bolivar had a daughter, who had been born after they escaped to present-day Maine. Twenty-two years younger than Simon, she served as an attorney for the Basque's in America. Named Lucia Maria for her aunt in France, the vivacious young woman saw Abe socially. Soon they became lovers. Two years later, Abe married Lucia, a woman five years older, in the Welsh tradition.

When Lucia Maria's older brother died in exile, Abe and his family moved to defend the outpost in Springfield, Illinois. Cornelia's contacts in Jamaica claimed that Simon Bolivar had been choked to death by infiltrators in the cause. Fortunately, his aide escaped during the skirmish at sea. O'Leary fled to Colombia with Bolivar's valuable documents and sent word that all was not lost in South America.

As the opium trade funded secret societies in major universities and Governor Wolf pushed for public education in Pennsylvania, Abe decided to run for the Illinois House of Representatives. Thomas Lincoln's group of traffickers captured Abe at the Dallas Scott property. Scott, a relation of Winfield Scott, kept Abe prisoner, while Wilkinson's agents created the Black Hawk War, like Madison had done with the War of 1812. They repeated the Patriot's ruse of the Boston Tea Party and dressed as Native Americans, except this time they ruthlessly murdered settlers and Native Americans. Lucia Maria, one son, and Mrs. Linkhorn died in the fray. Two other sons managed to run away to safety, whereabouts unknown.

Abe escaped at Paw Paw Grove to regroup with Captain Elijah Iles in Ottawa, Illinois. He joined Lt. Robert Anderson's militia there. Anderson's father had served as an aide to Lafayette during the American Revolution. His mother was related to Justice John Marshall. Anderson's parents relocated to Kentucky, where Robert became his childhood friend before Nancy Hank's murder.

General Atkinson attacked the garrison and captured Anderson's forces. Atkinson marched the prisoners to Dixon Ferry, where they revolted and ran for it. Abe and Anderson returned to Springfield. Meanwhile, General Edmund P. Gaines attacked Atkinson, Wilkinson's bunch at Kellogg Grove, and the traffickers at Apple River Fort. Anderson and Abe retook Fort Armstrong, named for Madison's Secretary of War during 1812, and established Rock Island arsenal. Abe destroyed any trace of his former family's home south of Springfield, in New Salem. After four days of searching, he found his sons asleep on a beach along Richland Creek. With Cornelia's assistance, Abe placed his two boys with a family in Bowling Green. After changing his name to Lincoln, he opened a store in New Salem and became postmaster.

The daughter of one of New Salem's founders, Anne Rutledge, later attempted to kill Abe in an alleged romance. Busy with the guardianship of his two sons, Abe eluded the poison squads. The hungry Roman gods demanded human sacrifice and cholera wiped out much of New Salem along with Anne Rutledge.

Resolving to stay out of occult affairs, Abe saw to it that the witch hunt hysteria of the Salem of New England could not be repeated by those company patriots intent on political leverage. He obtained a law degree and moved to Springfield, in time for the relocation of the state capital from its former home in Vandalia.

Abe served in the Illinois House of Representatives for twelve years. Toward the end of his last term, he entered a liaison with Mary Ann Todd, the belle of his friend on the debate circuit. Stephen A. Douglas changed his course and went for a woman connected to Dallas's occult lodges. Abe, holding true to his vow to avoid occult relationships, courted Mary Ann.

When they broke off the engagement, Cornelia decided to pay Abe a visit at his law office. Noticing the nip in the air hung in the autumn breeze, she tugged at her wool shawl to wrap it tighter around her. Then she hurried inside the main room. "Your boys enjoy school," she told him as he offered her a chair. Cornelia sat down and accepted a cup of tea from Abe. She continued, "Sometimes you have to fake it until you make it."

Still standing near the window with his cup of tea, Abe eyed Cornelia and put his cup down. "Lucia Maria and I never agreed with Simon's violent methods. My sister's death convinced me to come back and do my part."

"Marrying the Todd House will give you the cover that you need for the presidency."

"I've come to appreciate Southern manners," Abe confessed. "After everything that has happened, Mary Ann speaks to the hellcat inside me."

"Here are the latest designs for the Pentagon."

Abe took the papers from her hand and remained standing as he looked them over. He commented, "Simon spied on the Freemasons, but he was never one of them. He told Lucia Maria about the Scottish guild and their economic pyramids, which resonated with the number 3. The structure of the Pentarch is 5." Putting the papers down on his desk, he reclined in the chair behind it. Running his fingers through his unmanageable hair, he remarked, "I can see why the Pentagon wants a monetary system based on 4." He pulled a deck of tarot from one of his drawers. Perusing the cards, he extracted the four of wands and placed it on the table. "My gypsy wife always told me that a castle with four wands could always beat a Scottish castle filled with three norns."

"There lies the opportunity," Cornelia told him as she decisively rose from her chair. She instructed Abe, "Celebrate." Abe grabbed his overcoat and put it around her. As he opened the door for her, she quickly added, "Like hell."

He took a deep breath when he heard her. "I can manage that."

Then he went back to his desk and studied the tarot card. Shakespeare had placed the Three Goddesses of Fates, or norns, in MacBeth's Castle by the time Elizabeth I ran the seas with her pirate Drake. Though her half-sister represented the Scots, Elizabeth's sponsors came from the Pentarchy.

Abe murmured softly, "I'll let our kids run ponies through the White House in celebration, though their grandparents will want to dress them in Confederate uniforms. We'll even invite the Hapsberg side of the Pentarchy to come and dance."

Abe wedded Mary Ann and ran for the United States House of Representatives. After one term, he left to avoid conflict with the Todds over the Mexican-American War. After John Brown and the United India company moved to Springfield, Massachusetts, Abe began representing the state of Illinois in Congress. Some of the former slaves freed by his efforts in the underground railroad began speaking out. People like Sojourner Truth and Frederick Douglass foresaw the required struggle for freedom. John Brown's wool companies competed with Pierre's established cotton trade, which had involved many of Louisiana's colonial governors. Those in the business understood Brown's military zeal and opposition to the Avalon Queen von Fersen. After her murder near the Vogelbacher settlement in Pennsylvania, one of her daughters fulfilled the leadership position. Keeping the same name, she networked with the Eagles and a group of naval heroes known as Rangers. During the American Revolution, the Rangers had called themselves Roger's Rangers or the Queen's Rangers. The Queen in this instance referred to King Louis XVI's first wife, the daughter of Rousseau. Nobody sailed for Marie Antoinette.

A descendant of Vlad the Impaler, John Brown was out for blood. He suited the interests of the Transylvania Land Company. One of the financiers and signers of the Declaration of Independence had established a Secret Committee of Trade. The head of the Skull and Bones trade financed John Brown through the well known Secret Six. It was common knowledge amongst those guarding the Springfield Amory that half of the six were false positives. Forced to make their own guns and ammunition, the other half of the Secret Six set up shops for making Sharps rifles near Yale. After the Civil War ended, they manufactured Winchesters to win the West.

Ever since the death of his sister, Lincoln used his legal expertise to cultivate a local medical profession like the one that he had read about in his mother's books. As Rockefeller sold snake oil and founded the American Medical Society in Chicago, Abe continued to buy his homeopathic remedies at Diller Drug Store in Springfield.

"Thanks for lending me the book," the owner of Diller Drugs mentioned as Abe paid for the medicine. "The new school in Chicago will be seeking your legal aid."

"My wife and I agree on this issue,"Abe responded. "It is about the inevitable bloodshed, rather than the upcoming wars."

"The vampires are funding and arming both Blues and Grays," the owner commented as he handed Abe his package. "Hide these. The AMA prohibits its members from consulting with homeopathic doctors or patients."

Abe raised one brow. "Did you join the AMA, doc?"

"Not yet, but I am laying low until the pirates remove the leeches from the national interest."

"Now when have we ever had a national interest?" Abe asked.

The owner winked. He asked, "When do you leave for Congress?"

Abe chuckled and left the store without a further word.

When the British Government contracted with the Skull and Bones pirates for rifles in 1854, Abe mobilized the Republican party in Illinois as Captain Joseph Medill led the Ohio Republicans. When the occultists made it clear that they wanted slavery to expand in the states, Abe lost the Senate race to Mary Ann's former beau, Stephen A. Douglas. As Kansas bleed over the pro-slavery administration of President Franklin Pierce, John Brown's extremism reversed the political climate. Abe won the President's office for 1860.

Shortly after the election, John Brown attacked Harper's Ferry and the wife of one of Brown's Skull and Bone sponsors visited him in jail. The skull drudgery imported from Izmir, Turkey countered the arrangement of crystal skulls on the planet. Crystal skulls tracked benevolent airships and helped them land on friendly bases. Otherwise, they could easily be destroyed by those forces driving the refugee population to the planet.

Lincoln received word from Cornelia that their agent in Dallas, John Neely Bryan, had returned to Dallas after hiding with the Creek Nation. Bryan enlisted the aid of soldiers from Bird's Fort. Wishing to avoid detection, the soldiers had abandoned the fort in favor of merging their community with the Creeks. Together, they attacked the mind-control units of Dallas's settlement. Like the Erie Native Americans, most of the Comanches served the occultists and unwittingly took part in human sacrifice rituals.

Meanwhile, the former inhabitants of Fort Armstrong, which had been built on sacred Native American land, established large ranches near the Gulf. The Apaches tracked their movements and sent a report to Lincoln through Cornelia, who served as a cook at the White House. These ranches supported the trade interests of A J. Dallas and the Independence Movements in Puerto Rico and Cuba. An officer serving under Winfield Scott during the War of 1812, established Havana, Illinois in Mason County. Though he claimed to have recommended Lincoln for the job of postmaster in New Salem, the Ross operation countered the Annapolis efforts.

Chapter Fourteen

2004

"THE MEXICAN-AMERICAN War resembled the Yugoslavian War," Joe remarked, lifting a wooden rocker to read the manufacturing label. Restoring the rocker to an upright position, he told Tobias, "Like this rocker, many goods were made in Yugoslavia before the war. Yugoslavia served as a way station on the Silk Road and other ancient trade routes."

He pulled out a book from a shelf in his office. Opening to a header entitled Yugoslavia, he marked the page and handed it to Tobias. The flag of the region bore the Croatian coat of arms, a chessboard of the KGB during World War II. Croatia had been a vassal of the Franks, who pursued Salish law. The country made ties to the Byzantine Empire by striking gold coins in the customary manner of using images of local leaders. Whether by will or assassination, the vassals traded public officials for money.

The descendants of Pepin established trade routes both in Mexico and Yugoslavia. The Eagles sidestepped chess board politics by working with a benevolent group of intergalactics called Raptorgryphs. The Pink knights also communicated with these undeveloped birdlike creatures inhabiting a planet two galaxies away. Named Orin, the god of wealth amongst the denizens proved aggressive to both gods and mortals. He opposed only the mortals stuck in their third chakras, like ancient Greece and Rome. His opposition became known as Plutus, the ancient Greek god of wealth with underground connections to Hades and other progeny from Cronus. Whenever the Pink knights wanted to fight the gods, they asked the Raptorgryphs for help.

Descendants of the Pink knights eventually made their way to the Netherlands, where they joined forces with Joseph of Arimathea. Some of the early pilgrims found refuge with this group and ran a print shop. After establishing the Vogelbacher settlement in Pennsylvania, they came over on the *Mayflower*. The Raptorgryphs favored the Vogelbacher settlements, which retained their low Dutch heritage from the days of Joseph of Arimathea and the Alemanni. After the Hebrew insurrection, Joseph fled to present-day Belgium and Holland, where he stayed with the brother organization of Avalon, the Alemanni.

Joe purchased the rocker and placed it in the back of his sedan. Then he and Tobias left the flea market and drove to a gas station near Iron Mountain. Having left Michelle for half a year to investigate the situation at the airbase, Tobias looked forward to seeing his wife. She expected to meet the two men at the cabin rental near the lake. Tobias stopped the car at the pump, while Joe looked around. Before collecting his receipt from the clerk inside, Tobias watched Joe stroll near a hex sign on the wall of the garage.

The Pennsylvania Dutch placed pretty hexagon barn stars on their freshly painted homes shortly after the national currency had been shanghied in the 1780's. Some barns had the frakturs by as early as 1740, after the War of Jenkin's Ear. The term coined by the socialite rivals of the Almack, referred to the lack of manners that would be exhibited in the upcoming Civil War. The termed served as a calling card for the Dionysus cult, which sported a goat inscribed within a reversed pentagram. In 1740, members of the cult boarded a British vessel involved in the Georgia trade routes and needlessly sliced off the ear of the commander. The ear made it through various trade routes to British Parliament, where it was used to mock the commander. The rest of the world came to understand the power of the cult and how the nations worked together.

Intending to protect their homes and health in with a passover effect, the Pink knights employed an aspect of Metatron's Cube. Like the Vogels, the Eagles countering the Dutch West Indies traders made artistic representations of items important to their hearth, such as tulips, hearts, and alignments with the four directions of the planet. In this manner, they eluded the designs of Hera's owl on the US currency. Tulips, the Dutch equivalent of the Irish clover, signified the connections of the Trinity---mind, body, and spirit. After the Council of Nicea's created a reason to kill off the natives in Europe, the parties in Constantople formed a Pentarchy of the five major port towns: Constantople, Alexandria, Antioch, Rome, and Jerusalem. The push to bring the ideas of the Trinity in the Nicean code proved fruitless. Instead, they passed resolutions favoring the Dionysus cult. If kindness was what life was all about, then the occultists resolved to be unkind and undermined anything that mattered in life. They promoted materialism over spirit and anything else competing with the vampirish drive for destruction of the earth. Establishments such as Trinity Church or College became obnoxiously aligned with self-serving, materialistic interests blooming on Wall Street.

The owner of the shop noticed Joe's attention on the hex sign, which consisted of a rose compass. When Joe joined Tobias at the counter, he remarked, "It's 'chust (just) a pretty sign. There's several like them on the barns in the area. Keeps the KKK away."

Tobias pocketed his change with a smirk. "We can thank Alistair Crowley's influence for Huxley's addictions and *Brave New World*." Then he turned to the owner, and asked, "Where can I get one? If I put enough of these up, will it topple the chess game for the end of the world?"

The man nodded gravely. "It's a sign, but not a revelation for the Armageddon."

Without a word, Joe followed Tobias back to the car. "Didn't Crowley influence Pike, an organizer of the KKK in America?"

"Yes, the National Park system results to occultism to their other operations, the ones promoted by his relation, Zebulon Pike."

"I can see why everyone came to Iron Mountain to hide. I am not sure how the hex sign holds against a goat-driven herd."

When they reached Michelle at the base station, Tobias saw a hex sign at the landing dock. Pointing at the tulip design, he asked her, "Do those things really work?"

Michelle nodded and waved at a Raptorgryph hovering overhead. "Ancient goat gods don't like aggressive Raptorgryphs. They will do nothing against their landing ports."

"Do you mean that those huge Dutch barns housed Raptorgryphs?" Joe questioned.

"It's an old relationship," Michelle told him. "The inhabitants on Iron Mountain consider Orin as an assertive creature, rather than aggressive." Facing Joe, she added, "You have to be focused to exist on this planet. Some might call it aggression, but it doesn't fit Darwin's model for survival of the fittest."

Tobias stepped back as the five foot eagle with the ruby eyes and killdeer markings quickly approached. Michelle shrugged and Joe seemed oblivious to the bird dressed in Spartan armor standing beside him. In a deep low, silky voice, the bird explained calmly, "Like Zeus, I was one of the gods that didn't make it. I got stuck as an eagle, but the Andromedan artisans and I struck a deal."

Soothed by the sound of Orin, Joe ignored the physical presence and waited silently for more information.

Orin continued, "After the American Revolution, we took over for the fairies on the soul transport system. In the years following the French Revolution, we helped those seeking ascendance. During the Civil War, people made choices concerning their freedom. Now we are at the crossroads where evolution must be balanced with ascendance."

Tobias glanced at Michelle. "We have another wildcard."

Michelle commented, "It takes a while to assimilate the technology."

Orin added, "Plutus arrived after Gondwanaland began. His de-evolutionary aggressions handed the monetary system to the gods. Mortals die; Gods die out, especially if no longer worshipped."

Michelle walked away from the group and left the men to become better acquainted with Orin. Moments later, Tobias and Joe met her for lunch in the underground conference room. Vacant, except for the three of them, Joe felt free to ask more questions of Michelle. Instead of answering him directly, she handed him a book from a nearby stack.

Joe opened the pages of a book on Frederick Law Olmsted. Despite his proximity to a circle of wealthy dark occultists, Olmsted persevered after they murdered his mentor Andrew Jackson Downing. Familiar with the Art Noveau movement of Pierre Lafitte and the gypsies during the French Revolution, Downing and Olmsted put spirituality back into public spaces through landscape design. Olmsted friend, Charles Loring Brace, worked with Frederick Douglass on the underground railroad and helped with the network of runaway slaves and orphans at Iron Mountain. Downing studied Pierre's illustrations of Metatron's Cube and released United States terrain from the chains of the dark side. When Wilkinson, Zebulon Pike's sponsor, realized Downing's intentions, he targeted Downing in a steamboat explosion.

Olmsted pursued the path of health care reform and prohibited the agendas of the Blues and Grays during the Civil War. Unfortunately, he ended up in a sanatorium himself at the hands of the Grays. He remained their prisoner until he died. After the president's assassination, his cane was given to Frederick Douglass by Mary Todd. Like Downing, the couple understood the occult influences and took care to avoid their takeover. Lincoln's cane held the spirit of the nation. It was a spirit stick, blest by Sam Houston's contacts in Creek Nation. It represented the initial intentions of the Eagles to form a harmonious relationship with the Iroquois Confederacy and other nations. Though Mary Ann had set him up at the theater, she passed the spirit of the nation to Douglass, a former slave. Douglass had spoken at the Seneca Convention along with Susan B. Anthony and pressed the notion for freedom for all people.

Joe left his thumb in the book to mark the page, then he closed the book and stared at Michelle. Sitting across from him at the table, she put down her corn tortilla and explained further. Pausing to reflect for a moment, she assumed a lengthy narration.

"The President that we call Abraham Lincoln had a grandfather, who fought in the American Revolution. He was also named Abraham Linkhorn. He built a home across from his parents at Linville Creek, Augusta County, Virginia. In 1781, after the American Revolution, the Transylvania Land Company from North Carolina marched the Swiss Germans and Low Dutch to various stations in Kentucky. Squire Boone ran the genocide camps. Abraham's younger brother, Jacob, escaped and returned to Linsville Creek, where he built a home in 1800. Some of those at the camps worked the mines. Some of the inhabitants died and the locals cloaked their absence in mystery. When Boone's men murdered James Harrod, named of the Harrodsburg Station, the locals used poetic license in referring to the incident. They claim that he got lost in Jonathan Swift's Silver Mines. The Welsh became as the first slave laborers in the mining operations due to a long standing war between Wales and Rome. Often the murders were blamed on the Native Americans in the region. This served to make them the latest victims of genocide."

Joe rose from his chair when she finished. Abraham Linkhorn walked in the room. Handing a thick volume to Joe, who stood beside the door, he remarked, "Here's more info on the control panel upstairs. I find it with the documents that we sent with James Harrod. He sent the designs for the Pentagon to relations in the Mideast, after faking his death. Harrod left a bunch of bones in a cave for Boone's scouts to mistake for his own."

Joe examined the volume. Flipping the pages over, he pointed to a picture of LTC Rufus Putnam, the first chief of engineer in the US Continental Army. He served in the US Army about the time that Harrod escaped his tormenters in Kentucky. He commented to those gathered in the room, "I learned through my two-way taps that Harrod's documents showed up at the Mehun-sur-Yevre project."

"That's in France," Michelle remarked.

Joe blinked as he added, "During World World I, US Captain Somerville constructed a munitions dump there. Some of the US fighter pilots became lost in the desert. An Iranian prince, who wanted to help, gave them the Pentagon documents. The pilots gave them to the French pilots and they brought them to Somerville. Somerville took the instructions to Colonel John C. H. Lee, a relation of Jacqueline Bouvier. The British forces betrayed the Allies and something needed to be done for intergalactic protection. Both the French and Americans anticipated the alien's arrival, which supported the German occultists running the country."

"Somerville knew about the machinations behind Pancho Villa's operations as well as the alien extraterrestrial activities over New Mexico. Villa and his fascist allies intended to turn New Mexico into a New World Order. He replaced Colonel Lee's assistant, who had been captured."

"If the model came from Mexico, it would be based on terror and violence," Michelle surmised. "Mexico lacks a reputation for order."

Tobias looked up from the magazine that he was reading. He commented, "We can see how that one failed."

Joe chuckled lightly, "Yes, I've learned that many of their plans are not based in reality."

"Ever since the collapse of the pyramid civilizations, the area has been survived through chaos," Michelle noted. "The perpetrators are responsible for their own undoing."

"That is usually how it is," Tobias said, putting his magazine down. Rising to his feet, he announced, "I'm going on a hike."

Leaving the group, Tobias sat on the office porch and gazed at the rugged scenery. After a moment of reflection, he got in his car and drove down the mountain. He found an antique store and browsed the collection of hex signs. When he found one that soothed him, Tobias bought the item and returned to the mountain. He brought the hexagon with the tulips to the conference. Placing it on the table, he addressed Joe, "Check your sources to learn what happened to the Pentagon after Welle's pre-Hitler *War of the Worlds* in 1938."

"I already know that answer," he replied. "In 1933, Somerville conducted an engineering survey in Turkey and took a corporate lawyer from New York with him. They checked out the ruins at Goblecki Tepe."

Michelle studied the hex sign. After Pike's Federal troops abandoned Fort Smith, Arkansas became known as the Wild, Wild West. Descended from the families fighting at the Lexington Battle, Judge Parker came and restored order.

Joe glanced at the hex sign. "The Goblecki Tepe could have used a hex sign. The place is inoperable now. The men conferred with the sister civilization near the Caspian Sea. They ran into the Raptorgryphs there."

"Abraham told me that Orin works with the Pentagon as well as Iron Mountain," Michelle mentioned.

"After the War of the Worlds, FDR changed the location for the Pentagon and left the construction to the chief of engineers. The Hudson Bay Company overviewed the project before the bombing of Pearl Harbor. World War II became inevitable."

Abraham interjected, "The first chief of engineers established a munitions dump near Marietta, Ohio and Spoon River. Later, he became a judge in the territory. One of his relations served as a general during the American Revolution. Initially, he fought with Roger's Rangers, but helped Washington with the coverup to avoid being shanghied."

"By 1938, Germany had changed its design in favor of Zeus's Eagle," Tobias added. "The Secret Service was created to restore the US Treasury from the Roman Empire, but it became infiltrated before Grant assumed office."

Chapter Fifteen

"THE CARRYOVER FROM Abe's murder to John's concerned Pakistan," Abraham revealed. "Though the spirit of the nation went to Frederick Douglass and the Seneca Convention, the country was given to Pakistan."

He pulled another volume from the stacks scattered in the room. Opening the pages to the topic, he put it on the table for everyone to skim. Those from Narnia instructed the Rome Council of 500 to represent the will of the gods. Macaria, a goddess mentioned in the Suda, removed the United States from Hades's jurisdiction. As the daughter of Hades, she established a trading center along the Silk Road called Badakhshan.

"Badakhshan was BAD," Michelle said as she read the page. "The pronunciation must have degenerated to Pakistan over time."

"Shortly before the Dark Ages, they wrote the Suda in ancient Greek, though it is a tenth century Byzantine encyclopedia," Joe commented.

"You can see why Hades brought in Macaria," Michelle added. "He played her as an overture."

Joe paused and glanced at Michelle as Tobias continued reading through their distraction.

"Macaria took the dead as a blessing. Those dying before the Dark Ages missed Hade's damnation. It goes to show how she saw her father."

"She comes on the scene when courage endangers the living," Joe read, returning his attention to the book. "I suppose Abe considered himself lucky."

"Abe had inside information," Michelle quipped. "Have you ever read the last few pages of Master's *Spoon River*? The devils come and take them away. It became disgusted and put the book down. I know too many people like that."

Tobias smirked when he overheard her comment. Raising his head, he mentioned, "In contrast, the assassination in Dallas served as a time wrinkle. The populace grew weary of the bloodshed and rose to stop the Vietnam War."

"The Bay of Pigs proved another War over Jenkin's Ear," Joe remarked as stood upright. Pausing for a moment to collect his thoughts, he told them, "After the Czar left, American robber barons owned the steel and oil used to make the Cuban missiles. The pigs at the Bay of Pigs just wanted their stolen oil fields and sent their companies to take them."

"Sorta like Hudson Bay-United India companies and the American Revolution," Michelle said. "Oh look, here's a section on the Chateau Saint Germaine in France."

Everyone quieted as they skimmed the caption underneath a photo of the alien statue at the site. Germaine gave instruction to the Antient Lodge in England concerning US Constitution and other forged documents from the Eagles. Known from Atlantis as the immortal Sauron, his minions have taken over where he left off. His work later appeared as an altercation of the Hermetic Principles of Polarities. Hermes became upset over the application of his quantum level metaphysics reduced to the level of pool-table mechanics. Not every action in the universe has an equal and opposite reaction and this is where the mastery comes in. In quantum physics, some reactions fade or degrade exponentially. Every particle has a wave and that wave can be refracted, reflected, and harmonized. Hermes, the messenger of the intergalactic pentagon, brought a higher frequency to the Dallas assassination.

Not being a mason, member of the mob, or dealer, only one of those gathered in Dallas was there due to conscription. Nobody knew about the other's missions. Those from the army were angry at Oswald for marrying the daughter of the KGB general. He had crossed this proverbial line in the sand by betraying the Phoenician trade routes to the Pentarchy. Jacqueline had a lot of information on the Pentarchy and the man on the grassy knoll disobeyed orders. Though he was in the wrong place at the wrong time, he lowered his gun after euthanizing the first victim, as he had done in the Korean War. This in effect, betrayed the coup d'etat fashioned by the Napoleonic Federal Bureau of Investigation owned by Scottish occultists serving the Pentarchy. Like some of the others, they fled on plane to Hong Kong, one owned by the same mercenaries who had murdered young Joe Kennedy. Because the draftee had acted out of conscience and prevented a complete takeover, he arose as a hero amongst the military elite, who desired their freedom.

Never proud or boastful of his military roles, the draftee nourished a penchant for adventures and for seeing beyond the grand illusions of society. His view resembled an Apache shaman stuck in suburbia. His social commentary amounted to *the Protestants leave their empty beer cans on the back porch, whereas the Catholics display theirs on the front porch*. This perspective protected him and his family from the Dallas aftermath.

In 1963, Hades (Pluto) ley lines ran through Dallas. For those with positive karma, the affairs resonated with the Crosby, Stills, and Nash song stating *life is for learning*. In astrology, Pluto is associated with education, which is the best that one can hope for when in Rome. The survivors learned from experience and continued their work, regardless of the time dimension.

Without a word, Tobias and Michelle walked outside and sat on the porch. In the dusk, a cloud had enveloped Iron Mountain in a light mist. A woman emerged from the white haze. Fair-skinned, she wore a turquoise veil around her blonde hair. Dressed in brown suede leggings and a leather jacket without fringe, she lightly waved at them.

Stopping a few feet in front of them, the woman introduced herself, "I am one of Michelle's ancestors, the great-grandmother of King Arthur."

Garret Lynch appeared on the porch next to the couple, who stood to meet the apparition. "Tobias and Michelle, this is Lady Casper."

Michelle stepped forward and immediately hugged the ascended master. Having assumed a body, Lady Casper held Michelle in a warm embrace before extending an arm to Tobias and Garret.

"Great to see you again, Garret. I've come to take Tobias and Michelle to the Council of Elders."

Remaining on the porch, Garret briefly explained as the couple slowly walked away. "Lady Casper is an ascended master now. She doesn't die; she enters a timeframe and appears in the body that she had when she left. The Council of Elders meet in a cavity inside Iron Mountain. Enter their circle. They are ascended masters of the Arctos tradition."

Tobias and Michelle listened as his words faded behind them. They followed Lady Casper down several flights of stone stairs. Wisps of the vapor emanating from the cavity before them swirled over them as if inviting them inside with open arms. At the entrance to the cave, Tobias noticed Diana's falcon perched on a rocky ledge a few feet above them. The bird sat calmly as they crossed the threshold to the cavity.

Illuminated by an opening in the ceiling, the stone room appeared white in the moonlight. A small sputtering campfire in the center warmed the area. Crackles from the fire stirred Tobias and Michelle as if breaking a dumbfounding spell. A group of people chatted animatedly around the fire and greeted Lady Casper with a vibrant chorus of random statements. Lady Casper smiled at their attention and beckoned the others to address Michelle and Tobias. Uncomfortable by the crowd, Tobias remained stationary and took Michelle's hand. The group closed around them, forming a circle near the fire. Without anything to distract them in the center, the group stared across the floor of the cave at each other. Except for the sound of the fire, the noises in the room hushed.

"We are here to face the situation," one man began as he glanced at Lady Casper. "We are not celestials, we are a group of intergalactic time-travelers."

"Competitive forces and the dark side continued after the assassination in Dallas," a woman interjected. She stood next to Lady Casper. "Let's make an assessment."

Another man pulled a small notebook from a pocket in his leggings. "We are still hiding from Serpentine remnants." Placing a felt-tip pen over one ear, he flipped through the pages of his tablet. "Let's see. Neptune dissolved. The Lucifer-Hades-Pluto combo has been destroyed. Dionysus poisoned himself. Sauron and his counterpart goes in 2012; Cronus is scheduled to go in 2015; Zeus and the others have been put to rest...only Hera remains."

Folding his tiny book, he thrust it back in his pocket and gazed over the heads of those assembled and waited for a response.

"We gotta go after her owl on the US dollar," someone remarked.

"I have it," Lady Casper said. "We must not indulge her. Keep the hearth like an eagle's nest, while the rest of the home is made snug and cozy."

Tobias nodded in understanding. The parents built the nests in layers. One layer was soft, while the layer with the thorns turned inside surfaced when the young learned to fly.

Joe entered the cave with Abraham Linkhorn behind him. They crawled their way through a narrow crevice located at the other side. Joining the group in the circle, Joe produced a pentagram from his knapsack and passed it around for everyone to see.

"We found this along with the some documents concerning the intergalactic pentagon," Joe began. "They belonged to a cook in the White House during President Lincoln's term."

Abraham added,"The papers include the designs used byAnnapolis for the Pentagon."

Joe walked over to Michelle and Tobias as the circle collapsed into segments. He confessed, "I became bogged down in the analysis and couldn't explain until I found this pretty pentagram."

After spending a few moments chatting, the three friends separated and pursued discussions with the various segments of those gathered in the cavity of Iron Mountain. Joe proposed starting another intergalactic pentagon. Lady Casper intervened in the small talk and reminded them that there existed unresolved issues. The others in the area quieted to eavesdrop.

Though she had not heard the entire context of the conversation, Michelle spoke up. "Tobias and I can go to Galveston. We'll work with Lady Casper and the mustangs."

Tobias heard his name and moved forward to stand by Michelle. "We must get word out to the kids, so they can meet us there. They stay with their grandmother in New Orleans."

Lady Casper interjected, "Annapolis used the designs for the intergalactic pentagon, but the plans never morphed."

External disharmony reflected an inner imbalance. Internal changes would have brought power. Opening up to higher principles of order with the Council of Elders, the three friends learned to move forward without putting pressure on themselves. Tobias took a step back and thought about the task of reestablishing communications with the mustangs and Iron Mountain.

He whispered to Michelle, "The conflict with Hera is about cleaning house."

Michelle glanced at Lady Casper. Like an Eagle, the woman had learn how to overlook trivial details and leave the housecleaning for the intergalactic realm. Wiping a tear from her eye, she composed herself and smiled. She responded in a quiet voice, "Tobias, do you realize that the three of us have brought heaven to earth."

Never straying far from Michelle and Tobias, Joe overheard them. "In the *Kingdom of the Golden Tara,* the release of grief through tears brought us to perfection. What needs to be cleaned up is the world's notion of purity."

Michelle grinned. "That's almost an oxymoron, Joe."

Chapter Sixteen

1861

WHEN ABE WON the 1860 presidential election, Cornelia and the others ramped up their operations. Having relocated most of the staff from the Vandalia Hotel following Buchanan's election, Cornelia served as a White House cook and provided information to the president. Abe managed to defeat Wilkinson-Pike's agent, John Fremont while dodging Franklin Pierce's protege, Millard Fillmore. President Pierce, a company patriot, cut a deal with Buchanan to get him out of the county, so that he could not be a direct influence. Narrowly missing assassination by the Almack's rival, the Carlisle social network that ran the Court of St. James, Buchanan enjoyed incredible support from the Almack Club in Baltimore. The Almack in Baltimore coordinated its missions with the Peacocks and Eagles working at Annapolis.

Several days after Lincoln's inauguration, a young private from Virginia entered the White House through the back door of the kitchen.

"Oh there you are, William," Cornelia said as she motioned for someone to replace her at the cook pot. "The president has a note for you to give to his childhood friend at Fort Sumter. He and Major Anderson escaped together during the Illinois raids."

The young soldier followed Cornelia through the servant's stairwell to Abe's office. Looking up from his desk, Abe motioned for Cornelia to come in the room. Then he quickly rose from his chair and closed the door behind her and the soldier.

"Have a seat," he urged. "Thank you for coming, Private McKinley. My relations in Kentucky tell me that the Linkhorns and McKinleys remained great friends at the homestead in Pennsylvania. We saw what happened to the Erie's."

Changing the subject quickly, he told Cornelia, "We only have few minutes before one of my secretaries check in on me. I hired them so that I could give false impressions of my activities."

"The word from Annapolis is that we need to get this war going before we lose everything," Cornelia stated firmly.

William McKinley looked uncomfortably around the room.

"Agreed," Abe said, handing a note over to the man in uniform. "Tell Anderson to surrender to no one else but Lee. Give him my coded script. He's the only one, who can read it."

Turning away from those in his office, he whisked them away with one hand and ruefully ran his fingers through his shaggy hair with the other hand. Cornelia and the private left the room without saying goodbye. Hurrying down the stairs, Cornelia directed him to the kitchen where she filled his arms with parcels of food. He rushed out the back door with arms around his load and found his horse packed with fresh supplies. After mounting his steed, he turned and glanced at the lighted window of the president's office. Abe strolled over to the window and softly waved him off. Within a few weeks, war was declared.

Meanwhile, the Atkinson-Dallas network controlled the United India company from their newly built hotel in China. The Astor House Hotel, otherwise known as the Pujiang Hotel by the natives, connected with the evil yoga group in Calcutta, India. After losing the Battle of Cuddalore to the Eagles in 1783, these dark yoga masters worked with the company patriots. Responsible for initiating a time wrinkle that brought in alien ships from the intergalactic wars of ancient Egypt, the nazi-like sect took a new form. Before the American Revolution, a wicked guru had almost destroyed the entire British royal family by altering time. With assistance from alien airships, they destroyed the royal fleet anchored near the harbor. An Anglo-French scout named John Andre saved the King George's son and returned to England onboard an Eagle's trade ship.

The British United India company pursued John Andre until they hung him. Tammany Hall, also called the Columbian Order, took over operations at West Point, where Edgar Allen Poe maintained his spy network for Annapolis. Born in Carlisle, Pennsylvania, the Secretary of War during 1812 created an extensive ranching network along the Texas coast where they trained assassins. Working in conjunction with Santa Ana's forces across the border, they established trade routes supporting the Confederacy.

Shortly after Anderson's evacuation of Fort Sumter, Double J arrived at the White House. Dressed as a Union soldier, nobody recognized his slight Apache features. Cornelia led him straight to Abe's office overlooking the backyard. Assuming the posture of a sentinel, Double J slipped inside like he belonged in the room. The previous guard left his post for a much needed break. Abe closed the door behind them and nobody noticed the changing of the guard.

Offering Abe a new cane, Double J told him, "I bring Eagle Medicine in this spirit stick. Bilbo suggested invoking it, before the carnage begins."

Cornelia nodded and Double J continued.

"Starting the war now has given us the strong talons of the Eagle. The Eagle's talons grab what is needed, while the opportunity is within our grasp. It is the spirit of tenacity; the gift of clear vision; and the connection to the Great Spirit."

Abe accepted the cane, holding it across his palms like a treasure. He replied, "I appreciate your message from heaven. It could not have come at a better time."

After a brief discussion concerning the presence of Union ships off the Texas coast, Double J left the room. Cornelia hurried out of the White House with a note given to her by Abe. Going directly to the home of a socialite widow, the aunt of Stephen Dougall's wife, she entered the kitchen. Grabbing a tray for afternoon tea, she greeted the hired help as she sought Mrs. Greehow's presence. Her husband had died recently under mysterious circumstances, while working for the State Department in California. Buchanan's political adversaries remained a powerful voice in the nation's capitol. They pushed the Army of Northeastern Virginia to go after the Confederate capitol, so that soldiers such as Thomas Jordan could defect to the Confederacy. Knowing how Senator Calhoun surveiled Mrs. Greenhow, Abe sensed that the Confederate forces left in the town would try to use her. In his own script, he wrote a specially coded message to warn the widow. Having been orphaned by Calhoun's associates at an early age, she worked with the underground railroad.

Sitting by the fire, she read the note from Abe and told Cornelia, "Those wishing to serve the Confederacy are not leaving. I suspect that Thomas Jordan wants to move in."

"He may, until we catch him. Then he'll have to leave. Calhoun will tie up Congress with the inquiry."

"I can give them a lot to talk about," Mrs. Greenhow decided. "They are still mad at Abe about exposing the Philadelphia lodge's medical college in Pennsylvania. They named it after the man who rewrote the Eagle's Declaration of Independence for them."

"After they poisoned Eddy, he conducted an investigation."

"The lodge sponsored the same British company that contaminated the water at the Lexington Tavern, before the American Revolution."

"They later dubbed one of the signers *the father of American psychiatry*."

"Under Jefferson's orders, he set up Meriwether Lewis for murder."

"I know. They ran against Buchanan in the election for president."

"His student leeched Washington to death. In 1794, they took him to court for the Yellow Fever epidemic in Philadelphia. It became the first medical malpractice case in America."

"Abe represented Truett for shooting the man, who raided his place in New Salem. He worked with Atkinson and taught medicine to Booth. They started another surgery college in Chicago and named it after the malpractice signer."

After Cornelia left Mrs. Greenhow, she rode to Annapolis. By the time she arrived, the Army of the Northeastern Virginia had already been ambushed at the Battle of Bull Run. The son of the skull and bones doctor, who founded the surgical college in Pennsylvania, seized the remaining soldiers for the Army of the Potomac. His grandfather had served with the company patriots in Lexington and Concord. Jacobite by ancestry, the grandfather ran with the league of shadows on the Bunker Hill. Bache wrote about the infiltration his newspaper called the *Aurora* and identified the Jacobites as the illumined ones from Bavaria, Germany. This group pursued ancestors of the Linkhorns in America. It was for this reason that many descendants in Pennsylvania began placing hex signs on their homes, which served to preserve Pennsylvania.

A few tears escaped from the corner of Cornelia's eyes when she heard about the army encamped on the Potomac River. "They will contaminate that river for sure."

"We have already started a blockade of the Confederate's trade with Britain. Our vessels head for the Potomac now."

"The doctor that Truett shot has started armies in Galena, Illinois."

"The programmed individuals might be salvageable," one officer reasoned. "The natives tell us that one soldier appears fresher than the rest. He has only been there a year."

"What's his name?"

"Ulysses S. Grant. He drinks a lot, has a bond with the Confederate president, and runs with the devils of the Philadelphia lodge."

"Great. We'll send him where angels fear to tread."

"They are programmed to fight."

"He'll stymie McClellan."

Cornelia returned to the White House in time to see Abe's son succumb to complications from water contamination. Always hungry and thirsty at his age, young Willie disobeyed orders and accepted a drink from the coachman named McGee. A member of the Scottish Order of the Fates, McGee came as McClellan's guard in the White House. While Mrs. Greenhow went to prison, Abe and his family did their best to fool the nation that the White House had not been taken. Concerned about incurring the wrath of his own programmed soldiers from Galena, Illinois, McClellan stalled on the Potomac River.

Cornelia assumed her affairs in the White House as if nothing significant had occurred during her absence. She redirected her network to the hospitals, which Abe and Mary Ann visited. Bit by bit, they destroyed the Confederate spy ring along the East coast. Arresting a third of the Maryland General Assembly, Abe recognized the truth of the situation and addressed those who had already made their choices. He replaced McClellan and put a guard on McGee, though it required several replacements to get past the thick layer of human trafficking operatives at the top. With the Emancipation Proclamation, programmed soldiers like Grant began to reclaim their freedom. Lincoln encouraged Grant to run for the White House, in war and peace. Annapolis seized New Orleans and Pennsylvania stopped Lee. Eventually, General Grant gave up his horse *Jeff Davis* for another one called *Cincinnati*.

Meanwhile, the Philadelphia lodge shanghied the teachings of Phineas Quimby and merged it with New England Transcendentalism. Called the New Thought Movement, it realigned company patriots with the evil gurus in India. Annapolis considered the movement a threat because it brought the programming out of internment camps and into the streets of Baltimore. Corrupting the principles of metaphysics expressed in Metatron's Cube, the entangled mental constructs stymied the public far worse than what Grant had done to McClellan. Those traumatized by the Civil War became easily mesmerized by the theatrics of the Dionysus cult.

The Pentarchy reasserted its reach through theatrical productions, which romanticized gore and turned leaders into icons. Far removed from reality, holy war crusaders emerged on stage. Instead of accepting Lee's surrender, a cauldron of occultists invoked the Fates and brought in the Roman gods to play and toy with people's lives.

Chapter Seventeen

ABOUT THE TIME of Willie's fatal illness, several psychics visited the White House. Harbingers of the New Thought Movement, they attempted to get a foothold on intelligence operations. Cornelia ignored them and Abe fed them false information. Mary Ann openly grieved in their presence, finding it difficult to find comfort in someone named for both Andrew Jackson and Jefferson Davis. Having learned much about the intuitive arts through his first wife, Abe saw through the depersonalized readings and turned their interpretations against them. Mary Ann used them as emotional wastebaskets and eventually they gave up trying to be of service. Tracking the direction of their metaphysical forays, Abe successfully fought off other threats.

During the siege of the White House, General McClellan sent a marching band to entertain the president. The parade sang a recent revision of an old Southern evangelical hymn, which had become a popular eulogy for John Brown. While fighting in Kentucky, the army of a Scottish occultist named Officer Kimball presented the tune to the daughter of a wealthy New York banker. Married to a physician with the Greek Revolution, she rewrote the lyrics and published the work in *The Atlantic Monthly*.

"Mine eyes have seen the coming of the lord..." Tad, the surviving son in the White House, echoed one day.

"Now Tad, do you think that the soldiers are talking about Lord Russell?" Abe asked the boy. "He's angry about the Tsar's release of twenty-three million serfs. Alexander II is breaking Russia free from Hades and the Roman Empire."

Tad ignored his father and resumed singing with the armed forces. This time, he added his own words as he raced down the hall to avoid capture by one of the attendants. *"Glory, glory, halleluja, teacher hit me with the ruler..."*

The stalemate between Abe and evangelical bankers from Kentucky ended with Lady Casper's unannounced visit to the White House. Arriving in the autumn of 1863, a woman in turquoise dress entered Abe's office.

"Come in!" Abe jubilantly cried as he offered her a tray of Cornelia's biscuits. "I noticed the absence of the marching band."

"I came with the Russian Fleet," she said, helping herself to a biscuit. "If war is declared with Britain and Napoleonic France, then the admirals are under your command."

"What does the Tsar think about all this?" Abe asked as he sat down across from her. "Cornelia speaks highly of your role in the royal court."

"He decided to harbor the vessels elsewhere to avoid being trapped by Lord Russell's stooges in Poland. I am of no use to the royal court in Russia, so I directed the admirals to New York Harbor."

"I can imagine the euphoria erupting in New York," Abe responded. "It will spread to the Spanish-Portugese-French-British colonial empires in both Americas."

"True, that was the stated in the Eagle's original Declaration of Interdependence. Happiness is covered in the Constitution."

"As long as nobody kills Alexander II and me," Abe said, eyeing her with concern. Taking a deep breath, he added, "We can arrest the growth of such tumors as communism and fascism, though neither Grant or Johnson possess the clarity to pursue the Eagle's mission."

Lady Casper exited the White House and returned to the parties in New York. Meanwhile, McClellan almost died from typhoid fever. Ironically, two homeopaths saved McClellan's life. Though the Army Medical board prohibited homeopaths from serving in the military, McClellan never voiced any objection. Many of Abe's cabinet members supported homeopathy, such that he never felt surrounded by enemies. Abe defeated General McClellan and won the presidential election of 1864. The Civil War ended the next year. Britain depended on both the United States and Russia for over fifty percent of its wheat. Recalling how the price of bread had contributed to the French Revolution, England quit attacking the United States.

As the homeopaths and allopaths battled over war casualties, the district's postmaster general directed the nearby National Homeopathic Hospital. After an assassin killed Abe, the U.S. Surgeon General worked with the Secretary of State's homeopath to treat Seward, who had been injured by a man pretending to deliver a homeopathic. The AMA reprimanded the doctor, who saved Seward's life.

As surgeons hovered over the slain president in quarters away from the White House, several agents met with Cornelia in the kitchen. Scattered the petals of a red rose over the plowed rows, a casually dressed man Cornelia reported that Abe died long before being taken from the theater. Handing her an empty glass vase, they told her, "His soul found the flower that we placed out for him, just as expected. Then the light soared through the etched prism of the stained glass window above the rose. The spirit rose to the heavens above."

"Great. We saved Abe from some more torture by the AMA. Who did it?"

"The only ones who work on the Friday before Easter are the Romans, the counterfeit-money holders."

"The Romans came after Spartacus on Friday the 13th."

"We found the unsigned documents left on Abe's desk. The secretaries placed them there, knowing that he would be indisposed and unable to question the establishment of a Secret Service."

"It's no secret that they are of no service," Cornelia retorted.

"Abe saw the guard leave his post. The officer who questioned him said that he claimed to be with the Secret Service. By then, the assassin had already creeped into the balcony."

"The Secret Service let in General Booth's relation. They run with the Roman Empire and their medicine."

"It's the medicine of war and death. We must move quickly."

"Sherman marches to South America. He intends to go to Florida first. Grant intends to go after the Roman occultists. The homeopaths are replacing the underground railroad. The surgeons placed a bunch of morphine addicts around Abe. The AMA wants to do an autopsy."

"The Linkhorns and other family relations are leaving Springfield, Illinois for the West. We sent word to Iron Mountain. Lady Casper is sailing to Russia to rejoin the royal court. She estimates that she has another thirty years before the Roman Empire destroys the monarchy."

Under the moonlight, a uniformed soldier brought a horse for Cornelia. Packed with supplies, the stallion quietly waited for Cornelia's attention. She tightened her shawl in the cool evening air. Strolling over to greet the animal, she listened to the hushed whispers of the soldiers's voice.

"Stay away until the secretaries vacate. Annapolis needs your help."

Cornelia raced out of town, heading in the opposite direction of those arriving to mourn the dead president. At the crossroads, Cornelia slowed to investigate the appearance of a familiar shape on the corner. When Cornelia came close, the woman lowered her turquoise veil.

"They told me that you were sailing for Russia."

"A ruse to stop the attempted coup," Lady Casper told her. "Hades's daughter poses a lesser evil than Hades. Augustus Smith, the professor of Natural Philosophy at Annapolis, has a room for you in the District of Columbia. You were headed for an ambush."

Lady Casper climbed on the back of Cornelia's stallion and together they took another route into town. Pointing to the dead lying alongside the road, Lady Casper briefed her on the recent developments. Shortly before the attack on the president, the Council of Fires in the Tetons of Colorado signaled Iron Mountain about an incoming alien strike. The base station took a few airships down in the area that the Pentagon calls Area 51. The number five proved to be the lucky number and those hex signs in Dixie created a wobble in the alien flights.

Their conversation ceased as they came closer to the city. Cornelia tied her horse to a post and helped Lady Casper dismounted. The two women hurried into Augustus's home though the kitchen. They joined the rest of Annapolis's officers seated by the hearth. Limited to the light of the fire, Cornelia barely recognized the faces around her. Lady Casper began a brief discourse as Cornelia relaxed in an easy chair.

Annapolis had been carefully watching the arrival of Armenian missionaries from Constantinople since the 1830s. They watched how they controlled Confederate spies at the White House through the New York Press Club, a club founded about the time of the AMA. The president of the club brought in physicians to work with the schools in Philadelphia. Working with British intelligence, the newspapers directed the president's assassination. One of its members worked in the Lincoln Calvary, an errant group of horsemen employing the name of Thomas Lincoln for their own devices. Calling himself Joseph Pulitzer, the representative from Transylvania, fed the Confederate forces information. His network includes Jekyll Island, a debtor's prison funded by those responsible for the War of Jenkins Ear.

Shortly before the Civil War, a man named Hyde brought the Equitable Life Assurance Society to the United States. The oldest mutual insurer in the world merged the Roman's study of medicine with the financing of mortality. As double lives became more fashionable for those intending to survive the plethora of revolutions plaguing humanity, the skull and bones pirates from Jekyll Island collected data on private individuals. Once the information became available, it could be changed to match the pursuits of Jekyll Island. Inspired by the personality split of Deacon Brodie during the American Revolution, the masters of Jekyll's debtors prison funded both sides of the Civil War to create a split in the mental capacities of its lost colonies. Saying good is *evil* and evil is *good* undermines mental resources, which can be exploited by spiritual predators. We anticipate that someone associated with the Dionysus cult will eventually pen a script dramatizing Deacon Hyde and his Jekyll shadow.

Lady Casper paused for a moment before explaining the Mideast origins of Annapolis. She mentioned that the Scythian Neapolis served as the precursor for Annapolis. After Serpentine technology destroyed the caves of the Arctos, the survivors established Neapolis. After an insect-like race ran over Persia and attacked Neapolis, Alexander the Great released the Scythian prisoners. They operated the Silk Road and kept it slave-free. When ancient Egyptians began infusing occultism into the trade routes, a tribe known as the Caspi fled the Mithra priests. This group of magi practiced *medes* or medicine, which differed immensely from the military medicine of the Medici and the Knights Hospitallers. The Caspi worked with the Scythians, who obtained the information on Metatron's Cube from the Arabs. Pericles, the exiled leader of ancient Greece, had given the Arabs the best of Greek culture in exchange for refuge. In comparison, Alexander had learned what not to accept from his Greek instructors. Eager to learn from his mistakes, Alexander released the Scythians to reeducate the world. The Greek gods such as Zeus were not happy about their dismissal and sponsored the Roman Empire in retaliation.

Lady Casper stopped for a moment to rifle through the documents on the creation of a Pentagon. She displayed the building in the shape of a pentagram and passed it around the room. As others studied the diagram, Cornelia gave her report. Long ago, the design had proven effective in intergalactic wars. The only threat existed with a group of illusionists working for Hades.

"Though we managed to overthrow the snake-worshippers in India, the Mehrgar control this nation. They seized the Indus Valley after poisoning the minds of the Centauri. These intergalactic refugees settled the area in Vedic harmony and balance, after Serpentines destroyed their home of star clusters."

"The Mehrgar are related to Hades's daughter," Lady Casper interjected. "Slander is the worst form of poisoning, because both perpetrators and victims must live with it. The Reconstruction will be built on the lies of the American Revolution."

Augustus proposed, "Its time to split up the documents and hide them."

Underneath the present circumstances, everyone in the room agreed. Lady Casper took the plans for the pentagon to a shah in the Mideast. The documents from Annapolis went to Iron Mountain. In this manner, they separated the celestial from the earth-bound issues. Both realms found a new home on the planet.

Cornelia returned to her family, which worked at a hotel near the capitol. Avoiding the White House until the newspapers ceased sensationalizing the president's untimely death, Cornelia stayed near the hotel. She told her daughter to count her blessings, and that their choices had brought them closer to heaven.

BIBLIOGRAPHY

Dodich, Mark. *Fall Newsletter: Pluto Ley Lines in Dallas.* 2015.

Gray, Karen Cox. *From this We Spring: Family Stories Collected Once More*: Xlibris. 2014.

Morgan, Arthur E. *New Light on Lincoln's Boyhood*: The Atlantic Monthly, *February, 1920; Vol. 125, No. 2 (p208-218).*

Ullman, Dana. *Lincoln and His Team of Homeopaths:* The Huffington Post. Dec 23, 2012.

Vogel, Steve. *The Pentagon: A History.* Https://books.google.com. 2008. p11.

Wood, Matthew. *Seven Herbs; Plants As Teachers*: North Atlantic Books, Berkeley, California. 1986.